★

"Something wrong?" Elise shoved the chair under the table and grabbed her notebook.

"Yeah. A woman's body was found at the community college this morning."

Sam whistled under his breath. "Found by whom?"

"A couple of creative writing students."

Elise stared at Sam, her mouth repeating Debbie's words. "*Creative writing* students?"

Debbie blew a fast bubble from the wad of gum in her mouth, popping it with her teeth even faster. "Uh huh. They showed up for class at eight o'clock and their teacher was dead in a chair by her computer."

Her heart began to pound, her hands moistening around the notepad. "Did Mindy mention a name?"

"Yup." Debbie looked down at the pink sticky note on the tip of her right index finger. "It was a woman by the name of Daltry. Hannah Daltry."

★

Previously published Worldwide Mystery titles by
LAURA BRADFORD

FORECAST OF EVIL
JURY OF ONE

Laura Bradford
MARKED BY FATE

W🌐RLDWIDE®

TORONTO • NEW YORK • LONDON
AMSTERDAM • PARIS • SYDNEY • HAMBURG
STOCKHOLM • ATHENS • TOKYO • MILAN
MADRID • WARSAW • BUDAPEST • AUCKLAND

To my girls in Troop #2042:
Erin, Emily, Ashley, Madeline, Miranda, Janie, Savannah, Rachel, Olivia, Sonya, and Taylor. It's been my pleasure to watch you grow from little girls into young ladies. Never stop believing in your dreams…

Recycling programs
for this product may
not exist in your area.

MARKED BY FATE

A Worldwide Mystery/April 2009

First published by Hilliard & Harris.

ISBN-13: 978-0-373-26670-8
ISBN-10:   0-373-26670-7

This is a work of fiction. Names, characters, places and incidents are either the product of the author's imagination or are used fictitiously, and any resemblance to actual persons, living or dead, business establishments, events or locales is entirely coincidental.

Printed in U.S.A.

Acknowledgments

Once again, writing is largely a solitary endeavor. It means countless hours behind a computer, crafting a world from one's imagination. It means skipped lunches and late nights. It means staring at the walls while waiting for the right "voice" at the right time. It means way too many cups of hot chocolate. And it means a celebratory jig when typing the words, "The End" at the bottom of the last page. But no matter how much of it is done alone, it's never entirely without assistance.

My deepest gratitude to my best friend and writing buddy, Heather Webber. Without you, I'd spend way too much time talking to myself.

To my editor, Shawn Reilly, for knowing just what to say at just the right time.

To all my wonderful fans who have taken the time to drop me an email—your encouragement and kind words make writing Elise and Mitch a treat.

And to my "wind"…you contributed more to this book than you will ever know.

Thank You.

ONE

THE SECOND SHE SAW HIM, she knew she'd made a mistake. A monumental one.

Sure, she wanted to stretch her writing wings, but not beside the son of a man who'd been shot dead…because of her.

Elise Jenkins steadied her hand against the shoulder strap of her backpack and made a beeline for an empty desk amid a sea of grey hair and spectacles. Safety in numbers and all that good stuff.

But it didn't matter how fast she'd moved, or how many people she tried to hide behind. He'd recognized her, she was certain of it. The anger that flashed across his face, as their eyes briefly met, was all the giveaway she needed.

Jacob Brown may have come to grips with what his father did nine months earlier, but he certainly hadn't forgotten the part Elise played in the man's death. And that was something she'd have to face, head-on, if they were going to spend every Saturday morning for the next eight weeks in the same classroom.

"Isn't this so exciting?"

How she was going to face it head-on was another matter.

"Miss?"

Elise slid the backpack off her shoulder and set it on the floor next to her desk, her mind willing her eyes not to look backward. Should she talk to him? Try to make him understand? Apologize for the way it ended? What?

"Miss? Are you all right? You look a bit peaked."

"What? Oh, I'm sorry." Elise shook the troublesome questions from her mind and managed a small smile in the direction of the grey-haired woman seated at the desk beside her. "Don't mind me, I tend to…um…daydream a lot." She extended her arm across the aisle, gently grasped the woman's wrinkled hand. "I'm Elise."

The face peering back brightened immeasurably. "It's nice to meet you, Elise. I'm Madelyn. Madelyn Conner. I've been an avid reader my whole life, never going anywhere without a book." To demonstrate, the woman reached into her cavernous purse and extracted the newest Margaret Heights mystery novel, her fingers gliding across the cover with a sort of reverence. "Finally, someone at the senior center said I should try my hand at *writing* a book. So," she swept her arm through the air, "here I am."

Elise opened her mouth to form some semblance of a polite response, but the woman continued, her wide, pouty lips moving at warp speed.

"This here is Al. Say hello, Al."

A stocky man in his mid-sixties, seated at the desk

in front of Madelyn, turned in his chair and tipped his Yankees cap in Elise's direction. "Hello, Al."

Madelyn huffed. "This is *Elise*. You're Al."

Al smacked the heel of his right palm against his forehead and rolled his eyes upward. Elise grinned. Maybe there was hope for the class after all.

The man tugged his hat back down on his forehead then extended his hand and smiled warmly. "Sorry, Elise. I never tire of that joke. Besides, ol' bossy Madelyn here is fun to tease."

Madelyn Conner stiffened in her chair. "Bossy? How am *I* bossy?"

Al laughed. A hearty sound that echoed against the cream-colored cinder block walls of Ocean Point Community College's room number 41. "You got me here, didn't you?"

Elise sat back in her chair, her mind finally occupied by something other than Jacob Brown's presence in the room. Madelyn and Al were a hoot. True characters if she ever saw some.

Madelyn opened her yellow notebook and placed her pen atop a clean college-ruled page. "You will thank me for this, Al Nedley, you just watch and see." She turned her attention to Elise. "I've never met a bigger storyteller than Al. He could fill multiple novels. In a week. I figured it was my duty to bring him along."

Al shook his head, rubbing his stubbled chin with mock seriousness. "And the reason you brought Janice?"

Madelyn's cheeks reddened slightly as Al pointed out

the cotton-topped woman seated at a desk in the front row. "Well…Janice likes to try new things."

Al nodded, his lips turning upward. "And *Paul*?"

Madelyn waved away Al's questions, her lips closing together in defiance.

"Uh huh. That's what I thought." He looked at Elise and shrugged. "It's like I said, she's bossy. None of us seniors stand a chance around this woman. She'd plan our bedtime routines if she could."

If looks could kill, Al would be six feet under. Compliments of Madelyn Conner.

Fortunately for Al, the course instructor strode through the door, dropping a briefcase and a set of keys on a table in the front of the room. "Good morning, everyone. I'm Hannah Daltry." The slender woman of about forty-five stepped backward, perching her body against the edge of the table as her gaze swept around the room, studying each face before moving on to the next. "I daresay we have some great characters right here in this room." She pointed at Madelyn's friend, Janice. "If I were going to put you in a book, I would mention your erect stance. Maybe that small birth mark at the base of your chin. Or…" Ms. Daltry looked toward the back of the room, pointed to someone out of Elise's range of vision. "The way you're sitting, young man, with your legs sprawled out and your arms clasped across your chest…all things that could convey to my reader that you are angry at something. Or someone."

As heads around her craned backward, Elise kept her gaze on the teacher. She didn't need to look. Didn't need to see who had prompted the description. She knew.

"And *you*," the teacher pointed at Elise. "Your rigid stance, and the way you're forcing your eyes to stay focused forward despite what's going on around you, says to me you're either nervous, scared or guilty."

"I'd say it's guilt," snickered a voice from the back of the room.

Elise swallowed and looked down at her desk, her hands trembling as she clasped them together. Any residual doubt as to whether Jacob was angry at her was gone.

Al raised his right hand into the air, his voice booming across the room as the teacher nodded her head in his direction. "If I were to use *you* in a book, Ms. Daltry, I would describe the way you're leaned against that table, your head elevated so that you're looking down at us. Observing. Judging."

Elise pulled her eyes off the desk and stared at Al. Granted, they weren't teenagers, but still…

Hannah Daltry clapped her hands together, a smile stretching across her face. "Outstanding. And what is your name, sir?"

"Al. Al Nedley."

The teacher pushed off the table and walked around it, her hand grasping a piece of chalk from the silver tray beneath the blackboard. She sprawled one word across the clean surface.

Observe

"Well, Al. You may have found what I just did to be offensive, but it wasn't intended to be. I'm just showing you how to identify characteristics that coincide with various emotions. Providing the movements, the descriptions, the mannerisms of a character is so much more powerful than simply stating the emotion. Trust your readers to connect the dots. Always."

Al nodded. "So how would you describe me? What am I feeling?"

Hannah Daltry tapped her mouth with the index finger of her right hand. "I'd have to base it on your body language as your ball cap is shielding much of your face."

Al took hold of his cap's bill and began to lift it off.

"No. Leave it there. As you'll remember by what I just did, emotion can be picked up by body language."

Al tugged his cap back down and waited.

"When you first spoke, your arms were folded across your chest. Your chin squared. You were in defense-mode, quick to come to the rescue of classmates whom you felt I was treating unfairly. But now you're more relaxed. One hand's on the desk, the other in your pocket. You've moved forward in your seat. You're listening, instead of reacting."

Elise jotted notes in her book, her heart pumping with excitement. All her life she'd dreamed of writing a book, of creating a world from the ground up. And it didn't take a rocket scientist to realize that Hannah Daltry was going to be a wealth of information and inspiration.

The woman scrawled four more words across the board.

Write what you know.

"You've probably all heard that expression before, yes?"

Everyone nodded.

"What do you think it means?"

A female voice from the back of the room answered. "If you grew up in New Jersey, write about New Jersey. If you're a lawyer, write about law."

The teacher nodded. "Anyone else?"

Elise spoke, her voice quiet but firm. "If you're writing a sad scene, use a similar emotion from your life. It'll enable you to portray that feeling more clearly to your readers."

The teacher smiled. "Very nice, Miss—"

"Jenkins. Elise Jenkins."

"*The reporter?*"

Elise ignored Jacob's grunt, kept her eyes on the woman standing in front of the blackboard. "Yes."

"You're an outstanding writer, Elise."

Elise felt her cheeks warm as Madelyn reached across the aisle and grasped her arm, her smile set in a wide grin. "Elise *Jenkins*? Really? Wow, Ms. Daltry is right, you're great. I love your articles." She smacked Al's shoulder. "Did you hear that, Al? This is Elise Jenkins."

Al spoke without turning. "I'm not deaf, Madelyn."

Elise held up her hands, palms outward, and shifted in her seat. "Thank you. But journalism and fiction are two very different things—"

A chair scraped against the floor in the back of the room. "Oh really? I thought they were one and the same."

"I was right on the anger, huh?" said Ms. Daltry as she perched, once again, on the edge of the table and pointed at Elise. "What were you saying, Elise?"

Elise swallowed over the lump in her throat, wiped the moisture from her hands onto her pants leg. "Um, just that I have as much to learn as everyone else here."

"You're off to a good start though. You certainly have good contacts from your day job if you decide to write crime fiction." Hannah reached into her briefcase and pulled out two separate stacks of paper. "I'm going to cut you loose early today…with an assignment to help us get the ball rolling. I'd like you all to write a scene that shows some sort of emotion. Be it sadness, fear, apprehension, joy, or," she jerked her head in Jacob's direction, "anger. Put us wherever it is you want us to be, make us feel what your character feels. Keep it to a page and we'll read them aloud next week."

Hannah placed both stacks of papers on her table and stood. "Grab one of these on your way out. It's a scene I put together as an example. Read it, study it, absorb it. Then give me something even better.

"Oh, and don't forget to grab a class roster. I've only given the contact information you agreed to share when you registered for this class. You may find that forming a critique group is helpful. Or maybe you won't. It all depends on how you work. You'll also notice that I've included my cell phone number. Please feel free to call me if any questions arise. I gave you that number, rather than my home, because I spend much more of my time *here*—teaching, and," she pointed at a computer in the front right corner of the room, "writing."

In a rush, Jacob Brown was at the front of the room, a petite blonde by his side, each grabbing their pages and heading out the door, sullen and silent.

Elise lingered at her desk, slowly placing her notebook and pen back into her backpack as Madelyn chatted up a storm with anyone who would listen. She tried to be polite, to engage in further conversation with the elderly woman and her friends, but her thoughts were on one thing. Rather, one person. Jacob Brown.

Not wanting to appear rude, she forced herself to remain with the group, bits of their conversation filtering through her private pity party with buzzwords like "buffet" and "marks."

"Don't worry about the teacher's birthmark comment, you can barely see it," Al said, gently pulling Janice's finger from her chin. "It's not a big deal. We all have nicks and dings. You've had yours from birth. I've had mine since I disobeyed Smokey the Bear. Who cares?"

Madelyn abandoned talk of the omelet station at a place called, "Mama's" and jumped into the conversation. "I've got scars from my hysterectomy—you just can't see them very easily. Oh, and I have another, too," she hiked up her shirt and pointed at an angry red mark just below her breast, "thanks to spending too much time in the sun."

The man they'd referred to as Paul earlier pointed at a scar on his forehead. "Slingshot."

They all looked at Elise.

"Um. Well…" She flipped her hand over and pointed at a circular patch of discolored skin on her palm. "I was ready for my chicken pox to be done so I kind of helped things along a little."

Slowly they migrated toward the door, discussing accidents they'd seen and mumbling reminders to one another to pick up the assignment and roster.

"Miss Jenkins?"

She looked up, managed a slight smile at Hannah Daltry. "Yes?"

"I'm sorry if I stirred something up with that young man."

Elise shrugged. "You didn't. It's been stirred up for a very long time. Since the day I discovered his dad was a killer." She looked down at her trembling hands, her voice growing quieter with each subsequent word. "Jacob is angry at one person and one person only. Me."

"That may have been the case *initially*."

Elise turned, surprised by Al's words. "Excuse me?"

His left hand tucked into his jacket pocket, Al grabbed his papers and shoved them under his arm. "Initially he may have been angry at just you. But I don't think Ms. Daltry here earned any brownie points with him when she complimented your writing."

Elise opened her mouth to respond, but it was

Hannah Daltry's voice that spoke. "I suspect you're right, Al. Hopefully, though, he can find a way to tap into that emotion for his assignment."

Al Nedley headed toward the door, then stopped. "Let's *hope* that's all he does with that anger."

TWO

1:00 p.m.

SHE PULLED HER denim-clad legs closer to her body, rested her chin on her knees. The afternoon sun warmed her face in brief snatches, only to be shooed away by the near-steady ocean breeze.

March was still cold at the beach. Jacket-and-pants kind of cold. But there were signs that winter was losing its grip. The gloomy cloud-filled days were becoming less frequent, the air temperature increasing by a few degrees each week.

Elise dug her bare toes further into the cold sand and pushed at an errant strand of wavy brown hair that blew across her forehead. Other than a few brave sandpipers and an occasional pigeon, she was alone as far as the eye could see. And had been for several hours.

The amusement pier on the southern edge of town sat dormant, waiting patiently for the start of the summer tourist season in a little over eight weeks. She closed her eyes gently, tried to imagine the crowds that would soon cover every inch of this beach—people from all over the bi-state area flocking to Ocean Point for their annual family vacation. But she couldn't. It seemed a world away.

A slight vibration against her skin broke through her woolgathering, made her stop, focus.

Mitch?

She pulled the cell phone from her waistband and grinned at the text message icon on the upper right-hand corner of the display screen. Flipping the phone open, she pressed 'read'.

> **Hi Lise. Got here safely.**
> **Hope ur 1st day of school**
> **was good. I'll call 2nite.**
> **Love you. Mitch.**

Mitch.

The corners of her mouth tugged upward as a warmth emanated from her chest and spread outward to her arms and legs, toes and fingers. Even after ten months, Detective Mitch Burns still made her heart race, her palms dampen. He was everything she'd ever imagined and then some.

She smiled at the delicately placed diamond on her left ring finger as she pushed the corresponding number-to-letter buttons on her phone.

> **I Love you too, sweetheart.**
> **Have fun today. Be safe.**
> **Talk to you tonight.**
> **Yours, Elise.**

She watched the hourglass tumble in the center of the screen, her mind conscious of the one portion of his text she'd chosen to overlook. But if she told him, he'd be on the first plane home.

Besides, she could handle Jacob Brown.

She reattached the phone to her waistband and reached into her backpack for the homework sheet Ms. Daltry had given everyone. The assignment was simple enough. Tap into a raw emotion from your life and use it to create a memorable scene in which your readers experience that same emotion.

Curious, Elise began reading the teacher's example, the words sucking her in from the very first line.

The black metal cave was cool against my tears, the carpeted floor a buffer for the tremors in my body. I bit down harder on my lower lip, the pain a constant reminder of my need to stay quiet...to fight the urge to scream for help.

The end to Mommy's noises meant we could no longer hear each other. I was certain of that. But if I cried like I wanted to anyway, the men would hear me, find me. Maybe even hurt me.

I couldn't let that happen. I had to save Mommy. Somehow. Someway.

I hugged my legs tighter as I watched their calves pace back and forth, their steps getting faster and crazier with each breath I took. Two of the men wore brown work boots like Daddy's. The other man wore white sneakers with a dark blue squiggle, his laces coming untied like mine always do.

Blue Squiggle Man seemed scared. Like me. Every time his hands dropped to his sides they shook. Like mine.

Work Boot Guys gave Blue Squiggle Man lots of orders. Hold the bag. Stuff the bag. Close the bag. Watch the window. Hurry…hurry…hurry. If I were him, I'd tell them to stop being so bossy. Nobody likes a bossy Betty.

But maybe he's afraid. Like me. Or maybe he doesn't know it's okay to play with other people. His mommy should tell him that. And maybe she should tell him it's not nice to scare people too. I bet he'd listen. He seems to be a good listener. Like me.

A funny sound made them stop yelling and bossing. It sounded like a whistle or a—hey, I know that sound! It's a policeman!

I smacked my hand over my mouth to stop it from getting excited. Help was coming! Mommy and all the other people would be okay.

One of the Work Boot Guys ran by me, his feet smacking against the carpet real loud. The other one was next. They were really, really fast.

Squiggle Man ran too. But he didn't tie his shoes so he tripped. I've done that before. Only when I do it, I don't say bad words like that.

I bit my lip really hard as Squiggle Man's big body landed in front of me. Tummy first. He was tall, like Daddy. He wore a black mask and gloves like Dennis did on Halloween, only this mask didn't have a place for smiling or making scary faces. Just two holes for peeking. I closed my eyes really fast so he wouldn't see me.

I opened them again when I heard him making funny grunts. My grandpa sounds just like that every time he leaves the couch. Only Squiggle Man made his when he was pushing off the ground.

I knew I shouldn't stare, Mommy says it's not polite, but he reminded me of that girl, Sara, in the other second grade room. Maybe that's why he hung out with bosses. Because he didn't feel good about himself.

Work Boot Guys shouted at him to get out. Only he didn't stomp his feet. He just listened like always.

I sat real quiet after their noises stopped…just in case they were tricking me. But they weren't. They were probably too busy watching the fireworks.

If the policeman would hurry and get me, maybe me and Mommy could see the fireworks too.

She stared at the page in her hand, her eyes drawn to the power it wielded.

"Put us wherever it is you want us to be, make us feel what your character feels."

"Oh my God." The wind whipped the words from her mouth as she imagined the little girl who'd been so frightened, so alone under that desk. Was she real? Or was she simply the creation of a gifted writer?

Elise reread each paragraph, her mind playing out the image Ms. Daltry had created on the page. A child cowering under the desk. Alone. Without her mother. Criminals just inches from where she hid.

Could that kind of raw emotion come from someone's imagination? Or was it the memory of a little girl all grown up?

A series of quick vibrations against her skin brought an end to the unanswered questions that plagued her thoughts. Questions she hoped would be answered next week. Elise snatched the phone from her waistband and looked at the screen.

Unknown caller.

Disappointed, she flipped the phone open and held it to her ear. "Hello?"

"Hello, Elise? Elise Jenkins?"

The voice sounded oddly familiar, but she couldn't place a name. "Yes? Who's calling?"

"Hi, Elise. It's Madelyn. Madelyn Conner. From Creative Writing class."

Elise slipped the paper between her knees, held her empty hand against her exposed ear. "Hi, Madelyn. I'm sitting on the beach and it's a little hard to hear you with the wind. I could call you back lat—"

"That's okay, I can talk louder. See? Is that better?"

Pulling the phone a good six inches from her ear, she nodded. "Much."

"Good. I'm so glad we got a roster. Now we can stay in contact with everyone." The woman's voice slowed for a second, then resumed its rapid speed. "Have you had a chance to read Ms. Daltry's writing example yet?"

Elise's eyes dropped to the page flapping back and forth between her bent knees. Seventeen paragraphs that conveyed fear and innocence. Seventeen paragraphs that sucked you in and left you wanting more. "I just did. It was amazing."

Madelyn took a big gulp of air on the other end of the line. "I know. I never knew there'd been a little girl there that day."

She shoved her hand harder against her ear, strained to understand the words she was hearing. "So it's real?"

"Yes, I think it is. In fact, I think I know the event she is describing. It was a bank robbery in Paleville about thirty-five years ago."

"And you remember it?" she asked.

"Of course. It was the single biggest crime ever in that town. It was all anyone talked about."

Elise nodded into the wind as she waited for the woman to continue.

"Anyway, during this robbery, two of the three robbers were shot and killed. A third escaped without any money."

Shot and killed?

Pulling the page from between her knees, Elise's gaze flew down the page, searching.

I sat real quiet after their noises stopped…just in case they were tricking me. But they weren't. They were probably too busy watching the fireworks.

"Ohhhhhhh. The fireworks were *gunshots*," she mumbled under her breath.

"What did you say, Elise? I didn't catch that."

She shivered, then stuffed the page into her backpack. "I'm sorry, Madelyn. I was just thinking about Ms. Daltry's work. But what was that you said a few seconds ago? About not realizing there was a little girl?"

"The papers never mentioned it. They just talked about the employees and patrons who had been locked in the vault during the robbery."

Elise looked at the ocean one last time then pushed herself off the sand, brushing remnants of the beach from her jeans. "Sometimes the police leave details out. And with the safety of a child in jeopardy, I'd be more surprised if they *didn't* hold back a detail like that. But what makes you think it's the same robbery?" She balanced the phone between her shoulder and chin, reached down and plucked her shoes off the sand.

"If I'm right, Ms. Daltry is somewhere around forty-one or forty two years old."

Elise agreed as she walked across the sand toward the Dunes Road access point. Forty-two seemed like a pretty good guess.

"The robbery I think she's referring to happened thirty-five years ago. That would've made Ms. Daltry about six or seven."

Dropping her shoes onto the pavement, Elise balanced on one leg at a time, shaking loose granules of sand from her feet. "You know, I think you're right on the age. She said something about second grade in her handout, didn't she?"

"Did she?" Madelyn's voice paused for a beat before rushing to answer her own question. "Yes, she did."

So it *was* a true account…

"Have you started working on yours yet?"

Elise laughed. "No. I literally just finished reading when you called. But I'm sure I'll get started on it either tonight or tomorrow."

She glanced down at her watch, silently cursed the hours she'd wasted staring at the ocean. Print Right closed at two. There was no way she could get there, look at hundreds of invitation samples, *and* choose one…in under fifteen minutes.

Darn.

"Janice was working on hers when we talked a few moments ago. Paul and Al hadn't even read Ms. Daltry's yet, but that's not really a surprise. They're both fairly," the woman's voice dropped to a whisper, "*lazy* men. Then again, show me a man who isn't."

Elise grinned. Madelyn Conner was a hoot and a half.

The woman continued. "Do you have any interest in getting together as a group one day this week? Perhaps Wednesday or Thursday? We could all share what we've written."

She closed her eyes briefly, ran through the schedule

of interviews and meetings that dotted her week's calendar. "I can't meet during the day because of work, but I could do Wednesday night if that works for everyone else."

The woman's smile was audible through the phone. "Wednesday night is perfect. Six o'clock?"

"Six sounds great. Where?"

"There's a great little Chinese restaurant on Second Street. How about there?"

"Mia's."

"You know the place?" Madelyn asked.

"I sure do." She hoisted the shoulder strap of her backpack higher on her shoulder and continued walking. "Thanks for the invite, Madelyn."

"Thank *you*. For agreeing to meet us. I still can't believe you're Elise Jenkins, the reporter." The woman sighed in her ear. "I'll call everyone and give them the date and time. With any luck, Al and Paul will get off their butts and read Ms. Daltry's work. Maybe even bring something of their own to contribute."

Get off their butts? She couldn't imagine her grand-mother using an expression like that. Madelyn really was one-of-a-kind.

"Oh. Elise?" the woman's voice trailed off into silence.

She pulled the phone from her ear, saw they were still connected. "Madelyn? Are you still there?"

"I am. I just wanted you to know that I'm not going to invite that young man who was so rude to you this morning, so don't worry."

She crossed the street and headed south on Dolphin Way. On one hand, Madelyn's consideration would make Wednesday night more enjoyable. But, if she was going to get through the next eight weeks in the same classroom as Jacob Brown, she was going to have to find a way to deal with him.

"Madelyn, we need to invite everyone, including Jacob. If he doesn't want to show, he won't. But it needs to be his decision, not mine."

"Are you sure?"

Was she? Suddenly she wasn't so certain.

She breathed in deeply, willed her thoughts to agree with her words. "Yeah. I'm sure."

THREE

9:00 a.m.
Monday, March 28

SHE FLICKED ON the fluorescent overhead light, blinked against its stark contrast to the dark windowless room. Another Monday morning. Another kick-off-the-week staff meeting at the *Ocean Point Weekly*.

It's not that she minded the meetings, she didn't. In fact, she looked forward to them. Sitting at a table with other writers was always motivating, if not downright exhilarating. And, on any number of occasions, it even proved humbling. The talent present in this room each week was mind-blowing. A tribute, no doubt, to the instincts of their fearless leader, Sam Hughes.

Sam.

He'd been like a father figure from the moment she accepted his job offer, encouraging her efforts and believing in her ability no matter what the story. In turn, she'd learned more about writing from him in the past ten months than she had from all of her journalism professors combined. But, most of all, he demonstrated that her need to be a different kind of reporter—one who got the story without stepping on toes—was not only possible but appreciated. And for that she'd always be grateful.

"Morning, Elise."

She glanced back at the doorway and grinned, dropping her notepad and pen in front of her usual seat at the large conference table. Tom Miller's tall, athletic frame cruised into the room at his usual on-the-job pace, his cheerful smile a welcomed start to everyone's day.

Tom was one of those guys who seemed to buzz through life in a constant laid-back, happy-go-lucky state. But when it came to his job, he worked his tail off, earning the paper numerous awards for his sports coverage.

He pulled his ball cap off, tossed it on the table beside Elise, and ran a grooming hand through his thick black hair. "Any more burglaries over the weekend?"

"Unfortunately, yes." Elise smoothed a tiny wrinkle from her oyster-colored skirt and crossed her legs beneath the table. "The mobile computer lab over at the community college got hit last night."

"Wow! You serious?"

She nodded. "Got it from the intern over at the police station. The thief walked away with two laptops."

"Two laptops? *Two whole* laptops*?* That's the M.O. of a professional burglar if I ever heard one." Dean Waters strode into the room with his camera bag slung over his shoulder, half a bagel hanging from his mouth. "I mean open your eyes, people. He makes off with some prissy little Christmas ornaments from Ocean

Point Gifts two weeks ago, a handful of nothing-special watches from Merv's last week, and two whole laptops this week? Wooo-eeee. This guy's hit the big time. CHA-CHING, CHA-CHING."

Dean Waters was known for his unsolicited opinions and colorful descriptions, peppering most of his conversations with a witty, if not biting, sarcasm. But knowing it and expecting it didn't make it any less funny. Or any less needed.

The staff photographer had a way of pulling everyone out of their Monday morning fog prior to the start of the meeting. He was so adept at it she wouldn't be a bit surprised to learn Sam put a little something extra in his paycheck each week—strictly for his atmospheric efforts, of course. Then again, with as many interruptions as Dean caused during the actual meeting itself, *he* may very well be paying *Sam*.

Regardless, Dean was a smart guy. And what he said about the burglaries made a lot of sense. If the guy was a professional, the entire computer lab would have been wiped out. Prescription drugs from Merv's would have been missing. The Irish china everyone raved about at Ocean Point Gifts would have been gone. Not just two laptops, a few Christmas ornaments, and a handful of inexpensive watches.

She jotted a few notes on her pad of paper, thoughts and impressions to talk over with Mitch when he returned from Atlanta on Friday.

"Good morning, everyone." Sam Hughes pulled out

his chair at the head of the table and sat down, sliding four tiny white bags across the Formica-finished surface, each one stopping at the correct spot. "Where's Karen?"

"Getting a manicure? Harassing her husband? Scaring small children? Kicking a puppy? Take your pick. One of them is bound to be right." Dean unwrapped the top fold of his bag and reached inside, extracting a handful of chocolate donut holes. "But I'm good with that because a) she's not here, b) my ears get a break, and c) I get her donuts."

Sam kicked Dean's foot under the table as the photographer reached for Karen's small white bag. "Not so fast there, buddy. She'll be here soon. And, while you're waiting, maybe you could work to contain some of those incredibly warm and fuzzy feelings you have for your colleague."

Dean waved his hand in the air before plunging it back into his own bag. "Nah. If I changed my attitude toward Miss Society she wouldn't know what to do with herself, you know?" He plucked out three more donut holes and shoved them into his mouth, swallowing them in a single, dramatic motion. "Oh, and Sam? You might want to leave the sarcasm thing to me…your effort was pathetic at best."

She tried not to laugh, she really did. But Dean had a way of breaking through willpower like a wrecking ball. Hers always being the first to topple during a staff meeting.

"I'll keep that in mind, Dean, thanks." Sam opened

the navy blue folder in front of him, pulling out a sheaf of papers. "Yesterday's paper looked great, gang."

Elise smiled at her boss, waited for the individual comments he always made.

The wait was short-lived. "Tom, your story on the tapping of Rick McMahan for an assistant coach slot at Jersey State was fantastic. I didn't see anything about it in the Rob's River paper."

Tom nodded. "They haven't made the formal announcement yet, that's why. I got a tip and was able to confirm everything on my own."

"Who's going to replace him at St. T's?" Dean asked as he turned his bag upside down, searching for another donut that didn't exist.

The sports reporter rolled his eyes and scooted his unopened bag across the table. "Have these, I had breakfast before I got here."

Dean grabbed the bag and opened it in one swift motion. "Thanks, man, I owe you one."

Elise laughed.

"Got something to say, missy?"

She bit her lower lip and shook her head.

"Looks like you do. So out with it."

She knew it wasn't smart to engage Dean in battle. It always came back to haunt her in some form or another. But the material was simply too good to ignore. "I think you need to brush up on your math."

Dean's donut-filled hand stopped inches from his mouth, his eyes narrowing as he looked at her. "My math?"

She nodded. "You said you owed Tom *one*. By my calculations," she used the index finger of her right hand to tick off each finger on her left hand three times, "I'd say you owe him about fifteen."

Dean's mouth twisted upward, his eyes glinting in the light. "Actually it's *sixteen*."

Sam laughed. Elise rested her head on the table, mumbling under her breath.

"You better keep your pretzel bag close, Elise."

She turned her head slightly to the left and peeked out at Sam. "My pretzel bag, my water bottle, my computer, my purse…"

"That's a start." Dean popped the donut in his mouth and looked back at Tom. "You never answered about St. T's."

"They're not thrilled, obviously, but they've got lots of time to replace McMahan so I don't think they're terribly worried. Besides, the guy's done such a good job for them it's hard to begrudge him an opportunity like this, you know?"

"Thanks, Tom." Sam cleared his throat and turned over the top sheet in his pile. "Elise, I have to say your story on the little Morgan boy brought me to tears. That must have been difficult to write."

She looked down quickly at her hands, willed her breathing to remain steady. "It was. But Travis has more courage in that six year old body than most adults do. And if there's a chance to win this fight, Travis will be the one to do it." She swallowed over the lump in her throat, felt the tremor in her hands. "Dean's picture of him was amazing, wasn't it? You could sense the courage in his little face."

"You sure could." Sam reached for Elise's hand and gave it a quick pat. "You know I'm here when a story gets to you."

"I know."

His eyes lingered on her for a moment. "Did Mitch get off okay this weekend?"

"Yes, he did. He'll be working with the high school kids all week, staying with Jonathan in the evenings. He'll be back Friday afternoon."

"The department paying him to do this?"

She looked at Dean, surprised by the question. "No. Mitch is using his own vacation time to help Jonathan run this law enforcement camp. Why do you ask?"

Dean shrugged, wadding up Tom's empty donut bag and throwing it across the room toward the trash can. "I'm just surprised he'd go with these break-ins."

"There were only two break-ins before he left and he's in constant contact with the department despite his vacation status."

"Whatever." Dean balanced on the back legs of his chair and crossed his arms in front of him, the light shining off the face of his new black-strapped Timex. "How was your writing class Saturday? Are you the class pet already?"

She was smart enough to realize the sudden change of subject was Dean's attempt to lighten the mood he'd created with his line of questioning. Her gut was to change it back, try to figure out what motivated the questions in the first place, but she let it go. There was a time and a place for everything. The weekly staff meeting wasn't that time or place. "Class was fine. My teacher, Hannah Daltry, is an amazingly gifted writer."

"That she is. She's in my critique group and she routinely blows the rest of us away with her submissions." Sam shifted in his seat, tapped his pen on the tabletop. "As a matter of fact, we had a meeting yesterday afternoon and she mentioned your class. Said there was someone in there who was giving you a hard time. Is that true?"

Elise pulled her gaze off Dean and fixed it on her boss. "Jacob Brown is in my class. He made a comment, shot me a glare, but nothing I can't handle."

"You sure? Because if I can help in any way…"

The concern in his eyes was touching, it really was. But she needed to handle this situation on her own. "I'm fine, Sam, thanks."

He held her gaze a beat longer then turned his attention back to the list of weekly assignments.

"Maybe he just thinks you're hot." Dean grasped his hands together, rested the back of his head inside them.

She cast a sideways glance at the photographer, her voice a bit raspy, unsteady. "The only heat Jacob Brown associates me with is the fires of hell. But nice try, Dean."

As soon as the words left her lips, she knew she shouldn't have said them. A comment like that put men in protector-mode. And she was right.

Sam laid his paperwork down, Dean flexed his upper arms, and Tom leaned into her ear, his words hushed yet unmistakable. "Hey, if he crosses the line in any way, you let me know."

She held up her hands, palms outward. "Guys, I was joking. I'm fine. Jacob is fine. We're all fine. Please."

"You sure?" Dean asked.

She looked slowly at each man, her mouth turned upwards in what she hoped was a reassuring smile. "Yes. I'm sure."

"Cool, no spinach for me this week."

Sam snickered. "Dean, you wouldn't know a piece of spinach if it jumped on your plate with a name tag. And even if you did, you need a *lot* more than spinach to turn those sticks into muscles."

Dean gasped as he tried to pull an imaginary knife from his chest with Tony Award-winning theatrics, but the ensuing laughter was cut short by a yell from the vicinity of the front office.

Debbie.

"Good grief, boss, when are you going to get that girl an intercom?" Dean inserted a finger into his ear, jiggling it quickly. "It's either that, or free hearing aids for the rest of us."

It was hard not to laugh at the accuracy of Dean's comments. Debbie McAuliffe was the perfect secretary for a newsroom—efficient, dependable, hard working. But she also tended to get a bit excited about the story leads she fielded as a caller's first point of contact, that enthusiasm playing itself out in a decibel that would make a dog howl.

"Elise! Elise!"

She shrugged a question at Sam, pushed back her chair at his nod. This better be good…

Debbie's short, sturdy frame rounded the corner into the conference room, her eyes wide, her breathing heavy. "There you are…I've been looking for you everywhere."

Dean dropped the front legs of his chair to the ground. "Looking? I think you mean *shrieking*, don't you?"

Debbie rolled her eyes at the photographer in her trademark look of dismissal then focused her attention squarely on Elise. "Mindy over at the station just called."

Mindy Araya was the public relations intern at the Ocean Point Police Department. She'd been at the station for a little over three months and had taken a real shine to Elise. How much of that had to do with the fact Elise was the detective's girlfriend was anyone's guess. Probably a lot.

"Something wrong?" Elise shoved the chair under the table and grabbed her notebook.

"Yeah. A woman's body was found at the community college this morning."

Sam whistled under his breath. "Found by whom?"

"A couple of creative writing students."

Elise stared at Sam, her mouth repeating Debbie's words. "*Creative writing* students?"

Debbie blew a fast bubble from the wad of gum in

her mouth, popping it with her teeth even faster. "Uh huh. They showed up for class at eight o'clock and their teacher was dead in a chair by her computer."

Her heart began to pound, her hands moistening around the notepad. "Did Mindy mention a name?"

"Yup," Debbie looked down at the pink sticky note on the tip of her right index finger, "it was a woman by the name of Daltry. Hannah Daltry."

FOUR

12:30 p.m.

THE TREE-LINED WALKING PATHS were void of meandering students, the benches noticeably empty despite the sun-filled lunch hour. But it wasn't a surprise really, not in lieu of the tragedy that had struck the normally quiet campus of Ocean Point Community College.

Elise stood among the horde of students held back from the educational building by Troy Marcil, a rookie officer with the local police department. Occasionally a student would try to walk across the grass, head toward their class or the student center, completely oblivious to the police cars scattered around the area, but, for the most part, Officer Marcil had a pretty uneventful post. Uneventful to the average onlooker anyway. Torture, no doubt, for the policeman himself.

"Mitch is gonna freak when he finds out what he's missing." Troy ran the back side of his hand across his mouth then spat into the grass. "You talk to him yet?"

She shook her head. "Not about this, no. But I'm sure Chief Maynard will contact him at some point today if he hasn't already."

"Yeah, you're probably righ—hey! You! In the red sweatshirt! Step back onto the parking lot. Now!" Troy straightened his shoulders and shrugged an apology at Elise as he set off in the direction of the offender.

It was just as well. She wasn't there to stand around talking about Mitch. She was there to find out everything she could about her teacher's death. Pulling a notepad and pen from her backpack purse, Elise approached a young man of about twenty in a navy Ocean Point Community College sweatshirt.

"Excuse me, my name is Elise Jenkins with the *Ocean Point Weekly*, do you mind if I ask you a few questions?"

The young man shoved his hands into his pockets and grunted an affirmative.

"Do you know anything about what's going on?" She flipped to a clean sheet of paper and waited.

"Kinda. Some professor bit the dust at her computer. Least that's what my roommate said."

"How did your roommate find out?" she asked, her stomach tightening as she quoted the subject.

"Are you kidding? It's all anyone's been talking about for the past four hours. And what they're not talking about, they're emailing." He pulled a cigarette from his pocket and lit the end with a green lighter. "And you know what's kinda funny?"

She studied his face, noticed the hazy look to his eyes. Drugs? Alcohol? "No, what's *funny*?"

"The story keeps changing with each new email. Last

one I read said she'd choked on a stick of gum. The one
before that said she was tied up—bondage style."

It was obvious he had nothing worthwhile to contribute. All of his information was fourth-hand hearsay at
best. Thanking him politely, Elise wandered over to a
small group of women in their mid to late twenties.

"Excuse me. My name is Elise Jenkins with the
Ocean Point Weekly. May I ask you a few questions?"

The tallest in the group, a woman with shoulder-
length blonde hair, nibbled her lower lip inward and
gave a slight nod to her head. Her large green eyes were
red-rimmed, her nose somewhat puffy.

"Can I ask what you know about the events inside?"
Elise asked, her curiosity aroused by the woman's dis-
traught appearance.

"My teacher is dead."

Elise reached a hand toward the woman's shoulder,
gave it a gentle squeeze. "I'm so sorry. How did you find
out?"

The woman unraveled a tissue in her right hand and
swiped at the tears that dappled her lashes. "My friend,
Nina, is one of the people who found Ms. Daltry. I was
on my way into the building for class when Nina came
running out in hysterics."

Elise wrote as rapidly as possible, new questions
forming in her thoughts before the current ones were
answered. "May I ask your name?"

"Jeanine Voigt."

"Did your friend, N—" Elise looked quickly at her

notes, "*Nina* tell you anything specific about finding the body?"

Jeanine pulled a second tissue from her jacket pocket and used it to blow her nose. "Poor Nina was completely creeped out. It was hard to understand every single thing she said, so much of it was jumbled. But she did keep saying she thought Ms. Daltry was just asleep. You know, that she'd just drifted off at her computer." The woman's breath hitched as she paused briefly. "Then, when she touched her shoulder to wake her, she said Ms. Daltry's body was ice-cold and hard as a rock."

Elise's pen flew to the side margin, jotted an insertion note regarding rigor mortis. She knew enough from conversations with Mitch over the past ten months to know that full rigor mortis generally set in at about eight hours. And, depending on a number of factors including temperature, could last for up to seventy-two hours.

She glanced at her watch and mentally counted backward from the time the body was discovered. Considering the woman had taught a full day of classes on Saturday and had met with her critique group yesterday afternoon, anything from about 4:00 p.m. to 10:00 p.m. seemed a safe bet for the time of death.

"Did Nina say anything else?"

Jeanine shook her head, then stopped. "She kept saying it was freezing inside. That she couldn't get warm."

Elise listened without writing. An inner chill was something victims and witnesses often described in relation to a crime scene. Nerves, no doubt. And under-standably so.

She pulled a business card from her purse and handed it to Jeanine. "If you think of anything else, or you think your friend, Nina, would be willing to talk to me—call this number. Anytime." She put an arm around the teary-eyed woman and gave her a quick hug. "The police will move heaven and earth to figure out who did this."

The woman sniffed, her voice quiet and shaky. "Thank you, Elise."

"Take care of yourself." She walked over to the edge of the parking lot, scanning the notes she'd jotted from her interview with Jeanine. The case was fresh, just a few hours old, but she'd managed to piece together a good deal of information. The kind of information that brought clarity to a fuzzy picture. Ms. Daltry was working at her computer sometime last night. Odd, when you considered the fact that the community college was closed on Sunday. Yet completely in keeping with what Ms. Daltry had told the class on Saturday morning.

Assuming the woman hadn't died of some sort of natural cause, she'd been the victim of a crime. But why would someone want to kill a forty-two year old creative writing teacher?

She leaned against a tree, her thoughts running in circles. Who? Why?

The robbery.

She heard the gasp as it escaped her mouth, felt the

acceleration of her heart beat. Had Ms. Daltry's mere presence in the building been the reason for her murder?

Pushing off the tree, Elise shoved her notebook and pen into her purse and headed toward the car, her heart heavy with a realization too painful to ignore. Thirty-five years earlier a young Hannah Daltry had peered out from under a desk—too terrified to scream, too scared to move. Her solitary presence in that bank so long ago had stuck with her, affected her in ways one could only glimpse on paper. But she'd made it through that ordeal, lived to tell about it…until today. When, by a twist of cruel irony, she found herself in the wrong place at the wrong time once again.

FIVE

9:30 p.m.

MITCH BURNS HAD GONE over it a million times in his head, examined the choices from every possible angle. But it didn't matter. He was still at a complete loss when it came to the final decision.

Should he stay until Friday, follow through on the commitment he'd made to Jonathan and the kids in the camp? Or should he get the first flight back to New Jersey in the morning and take lead on the Daltry murder investigation?

"I understand if you need to go, Mitch. These kids seem to be a really attentive bunch which'll make covering things by myself a whole lot easier." Jonathan Moore moved the small rectangular cloth back and forth across his work boot, adding an occasional drop of spit when necessary. "I'm sure I can get one of the young guys to come over in the morning and help with P.T. and I can handle the investigative sections."

Mitch stared unseeingly at the coffee table beneath his feet, his mind processing Jonathan's offer. It was true. One of the rookies from Jonathan's old department could surely handle the physical training exercises. And Jonathan had way more experience in police work than Mitch did. But it was about more than who could cover which aspect. In the past two days, he'd clicked with the kids in this group, admired the drive they had to learn more about law enforcement. Sure, his leaving unexpectedly to lead an investigation would give them a taste of how life-encompassing police work could be, but sticking it out and seeing the camp through would teach them something equally important.

He glanced at the clock on the mantel and pulled his cell phone from his waistband. "I've got to call Elise, see how she's doing. Maybe hearing her voice will give me the kick I need to decide what to do—one way or the other."

Jonathan nodded, a smile pulling at the right side of his mouth. "That's what a good woman will do for you." He set his right shoe down, picked up the left. "Send my love and tell her I'll be seeing her soon."

"Seeing her *soon*? What are you talking about?"

The cloth ceased its back and forth motion momentarily. "Uhh," Jonathan cleared his throat, "you *are* getting married in October aren't you?"

Mitch flipped the phone open, his gaze fixed on the brunette smiling back at him from her place on the tiny screen. "We sure are. And it can't come soon enough for me." He studied Elise's almond-shaped eyes, high cheekbones, and whole-face smile. "Hey, mind if I sit in the kitchen to make this call?"

Jonathan waved away the question with a boot-clad hand. "Not at all. I wouldn't want to talk to my girlfriend with some old goat listening either."

"You're not a *goat*." Mitch waited in the doorway, certain his response would elicit a comment.

"I said *old* goat." Jonathan stopped shining his boot again, cocked a salt and peppered eyebrow toward the ceiling.

"I'm aware of that, sir." He tried to duck out of the way in time, but Jonathan was a precision shot— whether he was using a rifle or a pack of gum. "Jesus, what's in that stuff?"

"Old goat power, that's what."

"Point noted." Mitch tossed the gum back across the room and ducked into the dimly-lit kitchen, eager to hear Elise's voice in his ear. He missed her. A lot.

He clicked on her name in his address book, waited as the line connected and the ringing started. One…two…three…Double checking his wristwatch, his hand instinctively tightened on the phone as two more rings passed. Had she forgotten to tell him about a meeting she needed to cover or an interview she'd lined up? Or was there something wrong? She should have been home by now.

It amazed him how fast his mind jumped to the teacher's death and the fact that he was too far away to look after Elise himself. Even though it appeared to be a classic case of being in the wrong place at the wrong time, a killer might still be out there, free.

He was debating on whether to call the department and ask them to keep an eye out for Elise's car when he heard her warm, sweet voice in his ear.

"Hi, Mitch."

He closed his eyes, relief chasing away the tension that had begun to grip his body. "Hey, 'Lise. You okay?"

"I am now."

She was so sweet, so candid with her feelings. He'd never known anyone like Elise Jenkins, doubted he ever would again. She was one-of-a-kind.

His one-of-a-kind.

He leaned against the countertop, tried to imagine her in his arms. God, how he missed that feeling. "I assume you know what's going on at the college?"

She sighed softly in his ear, her voice tired and hushed when she answered. "I do. Mindy gave me a heads-up. It's so sad, so horribly sad. She was such a vivacious, passionate woman."

His stomach lurched. "You knew the victim?"

"Hannah Daltry was my creative writing teacher."

Mitch ran his free hand across his face and through his hair. "Ah jeez, baby, I didn't realize. I'm sorry."

"Reality is I knew very little about her. It's hard to truly know someone in the span of about twenty minutes. But she was so enthusiastic about writing, so passionate about what she did." Elise paused for a moment, her hitched breath audible through the phone. "She gave us a writing example when we left on Saturday. Something she wrote about an experience from her childhood. It was amazing from the very first sentence."

He pushed at an empty spoon cradle with his hand. "Chief Maynard was in touch within moments of the initial reports, filling me in on what they knew—and it looks like strangulation, though you didn't hear that from me. I know I'm far away right now, but you need to know I'm on top of this."

"Oh, sweetie, I know. In fact, I told a woman on campus that you guys would figure this out."

He felt a smile spread across his face. Elise had that effect on him. With just a few simple words she could make him feel like Superman.

"And we will." He exhaled slowly through pursed lips, the decision he'd been struggling to make becoming clearer with each passing moment. "I think I'm gonna head out of here tomorrow."

"What? Why? You've been looking forward to helping Jonathan with this camp for weeks."

He nodded to himself. "I was. And it's been great. But the guys in the department aren't ready for a murder investigation. I need to be there to make sure it's done right."

"Can't you just get the reports faxed to you there—tell the guys here what to do in the meantime? It's only three and a half more days."

She always made so much sense. Made him slow down, think. One more quality that fit with him perfectly.

"You feel okay without me?" He crossed his ankles, leaned his head against the cabinet.

"I miss you like crazy, Mitch. But if you mean whether I feel safe—yeah, I do. I truly believe Ms. Daltry's death was about timing. Whoever broke into the school to steal the computers wasn't expecting anyone else to be in the building."

"I think you're probably right."

"I just wish she'd managed to go unnoticed like she did thirty-five years ago."

"What?"

"It doesn't matter. I'll show you when you get home on Friday." Her voice changed, the quiet sadness giving way to an almost teasing lilt. "Guess what's in my hand right now?"

He laughed. "Saltwater taffy?"

"Mitch!"

"Like that's out of the realm of possibility?"

Her sweet giggle made him laugh again. "You know me too well, Detective Burns."

"Never *too* well." He pushed off the counter and walked over to the window above the sink, looked out at the blackness of the night. "So what *are* you holding?"

"I'm not sure I should tell you now," she teased.

"Tell me." He'd missed her the moment he had said goodbye at the airport, thought about her countless times since, but suddenly the missing turned to pure ache.

"Invitation samples."

"Awesome. Can't wait to see them. Can't wait to be your husband."

RELUCTANTLY, ELISE PLACED the phone in its base and leaned her head against the back of the couch. Three days apart seemed like a lifetime.

Her watery gaze instinctively sought out the silver-framed photograph perched on the wicker end table. The snapshot had been taken at the end of their trip to Mackinac Island, her uncle Ken capturing Mitch's face just as she'd accepted his marriage proposal—the joy in his eyes frozen in time, the raw emotion forever embedded in her heart.

"Oh, Mitch, I miss you so much," she whispered into the empty room. The words seemed to hang in the air, waiting for a response that wouldn't come.

She'd have given anything to have him home early, to be in his arms by this time tomorrow. But Mitch had been so excited to help Jonathan, so eager to spend time with a man who'd become like a surrogate father to him ever since they'd worked together on the Mackinac Island killings in January. The last thing she would ever do was get in the way of their growing bond. Besides, it was only three and a half more days, right?

She closed her eyes, imagined Mitch as he'd been at the airport Friday afternoon. Locked in an embrace near the security line, his aftershave had smelled so good, so enticing. But she knew it wasn't his smell that made passing women glance in Mitch's direction, two and three times.

Mitch Burns was hard to miss. Close to six-foot-four, his athletic body had looked oh so fine in khaki dress pants and a white button-down shirt. His hazel eyes had searched her face lovingly as he bent down to kiss her, their golden flecks twinkling as he smiled. In return, she'd run her hands through his thick brown hair, enjoying the slight wave beneath her fingers.

He was so handsome, so strong…

Inhaling slowly, deliberately, she willed herself to get it together, to turn her spiraling mood around. Pouting wasn't going to make Friday come any faster.

She pushed the tropical blue throw pillow off her lap and reached for the packet of invitation samples on the floor beside her feet. The selection was mind-blowing. Never in her wildest imagination could she have imagined how many different fonts, colors, details, graphics and borders there were to choose from in creating a wedding invitation. And, depending on the combination chosen, the resulting effect could be flashy, overdone, delicately subtle, or just plain boring.

She ran the pad of her index finger across the lace-like embossing on a pale pink card. The color was all wrong, but the detail and the cursive font were attractive, memorable. Definitely one worth showing Mitch when he returned.

In just the eight weeks that had passed since he popped the question, they'd managed to accomplish a lot. The ceremony itself would be held at St. Theresa's on the fifteenth of October with Father Leahy presiding.

The gymnasium of the school had been reserved for the reception and Mitch's aunt Betty was already in full-blown craft mode, determined to hand-make each and every centerpiece for the tables. Uncle Ken's fiancée, Sophie, had even jumped in on the preparations by volunteering to make the wedding favors herself— tiny scrapbook albums documenting Elise and Mitch's relationship since the beginning.

Choosing the invitations, hiring a caterer, and finding the perfect wedding dress were the only major tasks left.

She rubbed her eyes and yawned, the stress of the day finally taking its toll. Setting the invitation samples on top of the manila envelope, Elise stretched her arms above her head and squinted at the microwave clock through the pass-through.

10:54.

She grabbed the remote off the armrest and pointed it at the television. Another ten minutes wouldn't kill her. Besides, she was curious about the Daltry segment.

The closing credits for some cop show were pushed to the left side of the screen as Doug Fox, the Channel 5 anchor, appeared on the right.

"Less than one year after a string of murders rocked the quiet town of Ocean Point, another murder has happened here. Stay with us, News 5 at eleven starts in thirty seconds."

"Ugggh." Shaking her head, she grabbed for her purse and extracted a small blue notebook and ballpoint pen. She flipped the cover open and made a notation across the first empty page.

*Constant need to drag up the Fortune-teller murders even when the current crime has nothing whatsoever to do with it.

Was it any wonder why Jacob Brown was still so bitter? Healing was difficult when reminders were constant.

As she waited for Doug's overly made-up face to reappear on the screen, she said a silent prayer of thanks for Sam.

Her one hesitation about journalism had always been the sensationalism aspect of the profession. It was against everything she believed. But the drive to write and the drive to report had been so strong, so overpowering, she'd finally decided to see it through…under one condition. She'd never compromise her principles to get a story. Even if it meant losing job after job.

Fortunately, she'd met Sam, who believed what she believed.

"Good evening. The beachside town of Ocean Point, New Jersey was the scene of yet another murder this morning."

Hannah Daltry's face filled the screen as the anchor's voice continued. "The body of Hannah Daltry, a tenured professor at Ocean Point Community College, was discovered in an empty classroom this morning by two of her students."

The camera switched to a field reporter stationed in front of the building where the teacher's body had been discovered, nothing visible at this late hour except a few sidewalk lights.

"Good evening, Doug. I'm here outside the Flora building at Ocean Point Community College. Quiet now, this campus was teeming with police officers and bewildered students just twelve hours ago."

She kept her eyes on the screen as they switched to footage shot earlier in the day. One student after the other appeared on camera, eager to recount their relationship with the victim.

"Everyone wants their fifteen seconds of fame." The words escaped her mouth as she pushed the red button on the remote and watched the picture fade to blackness. It never ceased to amaze her how the news shows could reduce a crime—even murder—to an event worthy of front page status on a supermarket tabloid.

Her gaze fell on the writing sample Ms. Daltry had handed her just two days earlier. Without thinking, she picked it up and reread it for what had to be the twelfth time, the words just as gripping as ever.

"I'll figure out who did this to you, Ms. Daltry." She heard the determination in her voice, felt it in her chest. Journalism provided a unique platform for a lot of things, finding the truth at the very top. In her eyes anyway.

The ringing of the telephone snapped her thoughts into the present and she grabbed for the receiver.

"Hello?" She glanced at the clock in the kitchen again. It was a little late for a phone call. Except when there was bad news…

"Elise?"

"Yes?"

"Elise, it's Madelyn. Madelyn Conner. From class."

She felt her shoulders relax. "Hi, Madelyn."

"I just saw the news! Did you hear about Ms. Daltry?"

Elise pulled the throw pillow back on her lap, tucked her legs underneath her body. "I did. It's so sad."

"It's awful. That poor woman." Madelyn made a clucking noise in her ear, her voice taking on a higher, more screechy pitch as she continued. "I've been sitting here thinking what we can do. You know, to honor her."

Elise nodded, her thoughts half on the phone call, half on the background information she needed to piece together on the victim.

"Elise, are you still there?"

"What? Oh, I'm sorry. Did you come up with anything?"

"I think we need to keep our get-together for Wednesday evening."

Elise dropped her feet back to the ground. "What?"

"Ms. Daltry was passionate about writing. She wanted to make us think, reach inside ourselves. Like she did with her sample. I think we need to keep going."

Elise looked at Ms. Daltry's words once again, her gaze riveted on the opening paragraph.

The black metal cave was cool against my tears, the carpeted floor a buffer for the tremors in my body. I bit down harder on my lower lip, the pain

a constant reminder of my need to stay quiet…to
fight the urge to scream for help.

Maybe Madelyn was right. But even if she wasn't, what harm could there be in getting together?

"Okay. I'll be there. Six o'clock at Mia's, right?"

Madelyn's pitch softened, her smile audible through the phone. "Six o'clock at Mia's."

Elise set the phone down and stood. Sleep would have to wait a little longer. She had an assignment to write.

SIX

IT HAD TAKEN some doing, but she'd finally managed to track down a few facts about Hannah Daltry. Including her age, which Madelyn Conner had guessed dead-on.

At forty-two, Hannah Daltry resided in the same town in which she'd been raised. She'd attended Paleville Elementary School, Paleville Middle School, and Paleville High School. She'd left the area for college, earning a degree in education from the University of Maryland. After teaching at a variety of schools within a forty mile radius, the victim had finally settled at Ocean Point Community College twelve years ago.

Elise looked up from her notes long enough to open her top desk drawer and grab a handful of pretzels from the stash she kept inside. Not much of a breakfast eater, the urge for munchies tended to kick in around this same time everyday.

"You sure you want to eat those?"

"Why wouldn't I?" Elise shut the drawer with her empty hand, set the pretzels down with the other. Dean, as usual, had a built-in homing mechanism when it came to food, which meant he could sense the presence of it from about sixty yards away. Without fail. Once he found it, he was relentless until he scored a few scraps for himself.

"You sure they haven't been tampered with?" Dean leaned against her desk, pushed a strand of long stringy blond hair from his face and batted his eyelashes angelically.

She glanced at the pretzel in her hand, her stomach flip-flopping with a sudden dose of uncertainty. "You wouldn't…"

He lowered his camera bag to his feet and rested his palms on her desk. "I wouldn't?"

She looked from Dean to the pretzel and back again. Crud. "Oh here, take it." She pushed the tiny mountain of pretzels across the desk, her stomach gurgling angrily in response.

Dean's poker-straight face gave way to a devilish smile as he leaned over and popped all five pretzels into his mouth. "Anks 'ise."

If she thought she could get away with it, she'd have strangled him right then and there. With one of his prized heavy-metal concert t-shirts…

"Now that's not a nice look, missy." Dean pushed off her desk, picked up his bag and slung it over his shoulder once again. "Certainly not one you'd want Mitchy boy to see."

Elise pulled open her top drawer again, fumbled

around with her hand. Feeling the softness beneath her fingers, she pulled out a white paper napkin and waved it above her head.

"God, Elise, you are so easy to break, you know it?" he reached his hand around her body, took hold of the half empty pretzel bag, and pulled it from the open drawer. "Thanks, kiddo. These are yummy."

"Scram, Dean."

The photographer flashed a salty grin in her direction then disappeared around the floor-to-ceiling pole in the middle of the news room. It was hard to be angry at Dean for long. Sure, his brashness could drive the most stoic of personalities to drink, but beneath that ornery surface was a heart as big as Texas.

Unfortunately, Texas had just walked off with her breakfast.

Ignoring the growing hunger in her stomach, Elise turned back to her computer. The facts she'd managed to compile on Hannah Daltry thus far were fairly basic. The woman had never married. She was preceded in death by her father and older brother. Her mother, Genevieve Daltry, was a resident at Paleville Gardens—an assisted living facility for senior citizens unable to live on their own, yet not so sick they needed a nursing home.

She jotted Genevieve's name and residence into her notebook. Why, she wasn't entirely sure, but it didn't hurt to have the information nearby. Just in case.

"Hey, Elise!"

Debbie.

In the interest of the auditory health of her fellow co-workers, Elise scooted back her chair and headed toward the receptionist's desk, covering the total distance in less than five seconds. Dean was right. The woman needed a muzzle.

"What's up, Debbie?" she rested her elbows on the counter that separated the newsroom from the waiting area and waited for Debbie to answer the telephone and direct the caller to the right extension.

"Yes, ma'am, we received your subscription," Debbie punched a few buttons on her keyboard, moving from one screen to the other with a practiced hand. "You should start receiving your paper this coming Sunday."

Within seconds she was off the phone, eyeing Elise with surprise. "You didn't have to come up, I could have just told you what I wanted."

"That's okay. I needed the exercise." As cool as Debbie was, she hadn't seemed to figure out that her method of inner-office communication grated on her colleagues' nerves.

"Oooohhh, I love that top." Debbie jumped up from her desk and came around the counter. "And those pants are to *die* for."

"Really? You like them?" Elise looked down at her new pink ribbed sweater and charcoal grey pants. She'd swung by Short Hills Mall on the way home from Newark Airport on Friday evening. Desperate to buoy her spirits after dropping Mitch off, she'd wandered aimlessly past shop after shop, not seeing much of anything. The outfit had been an unexpected find.

"I love it. Has Mitch seen it?"

She shook her head, nibbling on her lower lip. "Not yet."

"He'll love it. Trust me. Hugs in all the right places."

She felt her face warm at the thought of Mitch and his trademark form of approval. "Thanks, Deb. So what's up?"

"Sam wants a sec when you can." Debbie retraced her steps around the counter and plopped down in her chair.

"Is he in his office?"

"Last I knew, yeah." Debbie shrugged an apology as she reached for the ringing phone. "Duty calls."

Elise waved and headed back to her desk, grabbing her notepad and pen before making her way to the walled office on the other side of the newsroom.

When she reached Sam's open door she stopped, observed the man seated behind the computer, his hands flying across his keyboard. In his early-to-mid forties, Sam appeared much older, his balding head an instant deceiver.

"Sam?"

He swiveled around in his vinyl writing chair, his pale blue eyes twinkling. "Good morning, Elise. C'mon in, take a seat."

She walked into the room, her gaze immediately drawn to the dozen or so plaques displayed on the walls, each one representing public accolades her boss had received for either his writing or his editing. The kind of documentation she hoped to earn for herself one day.

Setting her notepad and pen on top of his desk, Elise sat down across from Sam, her stomach growling loudly.

"Hungry?" Sam snapped a sizeable chunk from his granola bar and held it out in her direction. "It's not the best flavor combination I've ever had, but it's edible."

"I'm okay." It was a lie and they both knew it. The only food offer she ever sheepishly accepted involved chocolate—in either liquid or solid form. "Debbie said you wanted to see me?"

Sam rested his left foot across his right knee and leaned back in his chair, his gaze both pensive and curious all at the same time. "Anything on the Daltry investigation yet?"

She shrugged and flipped her notepad open. "Not much. The preliminary autopsy report isn't back yet. However, thanks to a reliable—but off the record—source, it was strangulation. I'll check in again with Mindy this afternoon, see if the official report is available. But regardless of *how,* it looks more than likely she was a casualty of a robbery gone wrong." Elise traced a figure-eight beside the notepad with a closed pen, her mind running through the bits of information she'd uncovered so far. "She was forty-two, grew up in Paleville, taught at O.P.C.C. for the past twelve years and is survived by her mother, Genevieve."

Sam nodded, his gaze fixed somewhere above her head—a look known around the office as "the thinking face." When he spoke, his words were pensive. "She was working on a novel, you know. A thriller. She was about three-quarters of the way done and it was spectacular."

She considered her boss's words for a moment, her thoughts quickly traveling to the powerful writing the victim had shared with Elise's class. "Let me ask you a question. I know you grew up here, in Ocean Point, but Paleville is what? Thirty, thirty-five miles away?"

Sam's gaze locked with hers. "Twenty-five. Why do you ask?"

"I realize you'd have been just a kid yourself, but do you happen to remember a bank robbery in Paleville about thirty-five years ago?" It was a long shot, but if she'd learned anything over the past ten months on the job, it was that long shots sometimes paid off. In spades.

He raised a fist to his mouth and exhaled against his skin, his cheeks puffing to twice their normal size. "Vaguely. Mostly what I remember is talking my buddies into playing cops and robbers afterward so I could run around and interview both sides."

She laughed. "Your friends thought you were crazy, didn't they?"

He shrugged. "Nah, they liked it. Less competition for the cop and robber roles." He leaned forward, his elbows planted on the desk. "So why the questions about a robbery from thirty-five years ago?"

"It's what you said, about Ms. Daltry's writing. She gave my class an assignment. To create a scene ripe with emotion—one that allows the reader to feel and experience it as if they, too, were there." Her figure-eights turned to tapping, her ballpoint pen bopping up and down on the top of her notepad. "She gave us a sample she'd written and it was absolutely mind-blowing."

She pulled her gaze off the pen, focused on her boss as he waited for her to continue.

"Anyway, if I'm reading correctly, I think Ms. Daltry was in that bank when it was robbed."

Sam's eyes widened, his eyebrows arched. "She would have been, what? Five? Six?"

"Seven."

Her boss lifted his hand from the desk, made a rolling motion with his right index finger. That, coupled with his thinking face, meant he was intrigued and wanted to hear more.

"While the adults were locked in the bank vault for the duration of the crime, Ms. Daltry hid under a desk in the middle of the action."

A long, low whistle escaped Sam's mouth. "If that's true, she must have been terrified."

"She was. According to the writing sample, anyway." Elise raised her arms into the air in an effort to push away the heavy thoughts that had weighed on her mind since news of the woman's murder. "I guess what I'm struggling with is how she got herself through a robbery as a small child only to be killed during another one thirty-five years later. Seems a bit cruel, doesn't it?"

Sam's hand reached across the desk, closed over hers. "Yeah, it does seem cruel. But you know as well as I do that Mitch and the department won't rest until they find justice for Hannah."

She blinked against the sudden wetness in her eyes, swallowed over the lump growing in her throat. "I know. It just stinks, that's all."

"That it does." Sam squeezed her hand quickly, then reached for the top page on his printer stand. "I thought you might like a heads-up. Your creative writing class will meet as scheduled on Saturday morning. Any chance you can help get the word out to your classmates?"

She took the sheet of paper from Sam's outstretched hands, her eyes skimming the email quickly. "*You're* taking the class over?"

"Yup. I was trying to figure out what I could do to help out. I thought the world of Hannah and feel awful about what's happened. Taking over her Saturday class seemed a good place to start."

She pointed halfway down the email that had gone out to Jeff Wilder, president of O.P.C.C. "This says you're going to do it for *free*?"

"Keep reading." He leaned back in his chair, his gaze, once again, fixed on the wall above her head as she looked back down at the email in her hand.

And then she saw it.

My only request in this offer is that my paycheck be sent to:

Genevieve Daltry
409 Maple Tree Lane, Apartment 2B
Paleville, N.J.

"Wow." She brushed the back of her hand against an unexpected tear that tried to escape down her cheek.

Sam waved his hand in the air. "It's nothing, really. I love writing—you know that. And it's something I can do to help. So, can I count on you to let your classmates know?"

She inhaled deeply, willed her voice to be as steady as possible when it emerged from her mouth. "Absolutely. A bunch of us are getting together tomorrow night at Mia's to talk about what happened and share what we wrote. I'll tell everyone then."

Sam flashed an appreciative smile in her direction, his eyes once again twinkling from within. "Thanks, Elise, you're the best."

SEVEN

THE HINT OF SPRING that had settled on Ocean Point earlier in the day was gone. The evening breeze was a painful reminder that winter wasn't ready to retire. Not yet anyway. Tightening her hand on the button flap of her jacket, Elise quickened her step as she rounded the corner of Cresting Wave and Second Streets, the brisk ocean breeze steady against her face.

Just one more block...

"Mother Nature sure is having the last laugh, isn't she?"

Startled, Elise swung her head to the left as a stocky, grey-haired man emerged from a parked car, popped two coins into a meter, and stepped onto the sidewalk just inches away. He was followed closely behind by another man—this one with a wide swath of shiny skin running interference through tufts of coarse, white hair.

"Oh hey, I'm sorry, Elise. It's me, Al. From class, remember?" The tall, stocky man pulled a Yankees cap from his back pocket and positioned it over his thick hair with a practiced hand. "That better?"

She grinned, her cheeks warming rapidly despite the persistent, cold wind. "Of course. I'm sorry. I guess I just didn't recognize you without the cap." She held her hand out to the second man, winced as he shook it with an unexpected strength. "You're Paul, aren't you?"

The man nodded. "Yep."

Al jammed his hands into his pockets, rolling his eyes as he leaned closer to Elise. "Don't mind him, he doesn't say much."

"Thanks for the tip." She pulled the flap of her jacket closer, her teeth starting to chatter. "Going to Mia's, right?"

Al tugged the right side of his coat open and chin-pointed at the bi-folded paper jutting from his inside breast pocket. "Got my assignment right here. I figured if I didn't bring something I'd pay for it with sore ears."

She arched a questioning eyebrow. "Sore ears?"

"You heard Madelyn. The woman talks non-stop. And if you get her dander up…well, let's just say it's not real pretty." Al motioned down the street with his right hand. "Shall we?"

"Please." She fell into step with the men, eager to seek shelter as quickly as possible.

As she expected, Mia's place was warm and inviting, an aromatic mixture of soy sauce and teriyaki hovering in the air above the intermittent laughter and hushed chatter.

Mia looked up from the register when the door-tripped bell announced their arrival. "Ohhhh, Ewise. It good to see you." The woman called out to someone in the kitchen then came around the counter, grasping Elise's hands in her own. "You cold, so cold." Mia let go of Elise's left hand and sandwiched her right one, gently rubbing until some much-needed warmth returned. "Ohhhh that better. Now let's take care of the other."

She could feel the day's tension dissipating from her body as Mia worked on her hands. It was a comforting feeling, a comforting place. "Thank you, Mia. It's getting so cold outside."

The woman nodded quickly. "Yes, it is." She darted her head around Elise's shoulder, her gently-lined brow furrowing ever so slightly. "Where Mitch today?"

Elise turned her hand inside Mia's grasp and squeezed gently, reassuringly. "Mitch is fine. He's in Georgia working at a law enforcement camp for high school kids. He'll be home on Friday."

Mia's shoulders relaxed, the corners of her mouth pushing upward. "Good. Good. I bet you miss him, no?"

She blinked against the sudden sting in her eyes, opted to nod rather than answer for fear her voice would crack. But it didn't matter, Mia knew. She always knew.

"He miss you too, Ewise."

She inhaled deeply, willed herself to focus on something other than her fiancé. "Mia, I'd like you to meet my friends, Al Nedley and Paul—I'm sorry, I don't know your last name, Paul."

Paul shrugged, his voice muffled. "Jordan."

Al stepped forward, pulled his right hand from his pocket and grasped Mia's. "Nice to meet you, Mia. I've heard amazing things about your food."

Mia bowed her head quickly, her lips twitching ever so slightly as a flash of color played on her pale cheeks. "I hope you tink so too."

The woman backed her way toward the line of customers placing orders with a frazzled looking cook. "I do work now. Ewise, egg roll, pepper steak and white rice?"

"You know me too well, Mia."

"You good girl, Ewise. Now, sit. I bring to you. You pay later."

She mouthed a thank you as the woman returned to her place behind the register.

"She seems sweet," Al said, his voice barely above a whisper. "I'm sorry Paul is such a stick in the mud."

"It's okay." Elise motioned to the plastic holder on the side of the counter. "The menus are right there. Once you know what you want, you order and pay here, then Mia will bring your food out when it's ready."

"Sounds good. Paul? You gonna order something?"

She didn't stick around to hear the man's grunted response, choosing instead to head back to the dining room and find a place to sit. The restaurant was jumping, people eating at nearly every table. It was official. Word had gotten out. Mia's once quiet establishment was now the place to be. Especially on a cold, breezy night like this one.

It wasn't hard to pick out the critique group among the regular customers. Four square tables had been pushed together in the front left corner of the room, backpacks, briefcases, and purses lining the nearest wall. Madelyn Conner was in the middle of the mix, her elevated voice and *tsking* sounds a giveaway to the conversation Elise wasn't quite close enough to hear.

If they read and critiqued the work of even half the group, it would be an accomplishment. Especially when the murder of their teacher was sure to be on the minds and lips of everyone there.

Her eyes skirted the room, stopped briefly on the table she'd sat at with Mitch last summer—a chance meeting over dinner that had exploded into a relationship neither could live without. A relationship that would soon be for life.

She slid her hands down the front flap of her coat, unbuttoning it as she went, her mental clock counting the hours until he returned. She waved to a city councilmember, smiled at the local librarian, but it was the pair hunched over a computer screen in the back right corner that made her pause.

Dean?

Nah, it couldn't be. For two reasons. First, Dean's women weren't usually quite so cute. Second, Dean didn't do computers—or, as he referred to them—the Satan of modern society.

Bobbing her head to the side, she squinted across the dimly lit room, confident her eyes were playing tricks, bleary from another night of restless dreams.

It was still Dean, all right. His stringy blond hair was pulled back into a low ponytail, his scrawny body decked out in a black Iron Maiden t-shirt and his face scrunched in confusion.

But who was the girl? And, more importantly, how did Elise know her?

"Oh, look, Elise is here. Elise! Elise! Over here."

The sound of her name ricocheted through her brain, pulling her focus from Dean and onto the group she was there to meet. She veered to the left and waved at Madelyn.

"I saved a spot for you right here." The woman patted the vacant seat beside her own. "Just about everyone is here, except, of course, Al and Paul and—"

"Oh no, they're here. They're up front ordering." Elise draped her coat over the back of her chair and sat down, greeting each of the other students with a nod and a smile before looking back at Madelyn. "What about Jacob, is he coming?"

"As a matter of fact, he *is*. That's not a problem for you, is it?"

Elise looked up, surprised by the unfamiliar voice and the tension it held.

The girl who had been sitting with Dean.

Suddenly a piece of the puzzle was in place. The girl with the shoulder-length blonde hair was the same girl she'd seen in class on Saturday. With Jacob Brown.

"Of course it's not a problem. It's why I was asking." Elise extended her hand. "We haven't met yet, I'm Elise."

The girl's emerald green eyes widened in momentary surprise, her voice raspy and uncertain as it emerged from her lips. "I, um…" She glanced down at the floor, shifted from foot to foot, then shyly offered her hand in return, pulling it back just as quickly as it had been given. "I'm Sierra…McDermott."

"It's nice to meet you, Sierra. I see we have a mutual friend."

Sierra's eyebrows furrowed, her nostril flared. "I don't think Jacob considers you a fr—"

Elise shook her head. "I wasn't referring to Jacob, though, from what I remember of him the few times we met last summer, he's a very nice guy too." Elise forced her smile to remain strong despite knowing that all eyes were on them, all ears perked forward waiting for some sort of dirt. "But I meant Dean."

"Dean? Who's Dean?" The girl glanced across the room as she spoke, her body tensing. "Forget it, I gotta sit down."

Sierra moved around the table like lightning, her body sliding into one of two empty seats at the far side of the table.

"What on earth?" Madelyn leaned into Elise's arm, her voice surprisingly quiet.

But the reason for the girl's sudden scurry became crystal clear before Elise had finished her shrug. Al and Paul sauntered into the dining room, Jacob Brown on their heels, words like "baseball," "spring training," and "pitching staff" permeating the air. This Jacob was happy and animated, as distant from Saturday's Jacob as one could imagine.

He walked over to the table, stopping behind Sierra's seat. "Hey there, beautiful."

Elise tried not to stare as Sierra's face lit from within, her eyes dancing as she looked up at her boyfriend. Jacob leaned over, planted a kiss on Sierra's hair, and sat in the vacant seat to her left, Paul and Al taking seats beside him.

She watched as Jacob pulled his backpack onto his lap, unzipped the top, and foraged around inside, finally extracting a dark blue folder before dropping his bag to the ground. "Ms. Daltry is, I mean, *was,* one helluva writer. Wasn't she?"

Everyone agreed.

It was hard to rationalize the enormous change in the personality of the young man sitting at the other end of the table, but maybe he was trying to be civil, to let bygones be bygones. Or maybe he simply hadn't noticed her yet.

"Isn't it just awful, what happened to her? I can't imagine anyone wanting to hurt someone like that." Madelyn inhaled dramatically, her hands intertwining with one another. "I sure hope they catch the person responsible."

Heads bobbed again.

"And to think, Al over there actually did his assignment." Madelyn straightened her back. "That's kind of why I wanted to get together tonight. I know our class is over now, but I thought maybe we could share our work with everyone this one time."

"Actually, our class *isn't* over. A replacement teacher has been assigned to our class and we'll meet as scheduled on Saturday morning." Elise crossed her legs under the table, looking slowly at each student seated around the table, her gaze coming to rest on Jacob.

Bygones were certainly not bygones. One only had to see his eyes at the moment of direct contact to know that. But he was making an effort and an effort was better than nothing. Baby steps and all that stuff...

"No one told me that," Madelyn said, her voice bordering on huffy.

Elise waved her hand quickly. "It was just firmed up yesterday, and I volunteered to tell everyone since we were getting together anyway."

"Well who, then?"

"Sam Hughes."

"Who's Sam Hughes?" Al pulled his ball cap off and reached for a glass of soda. "And is Sam a guy or a girl?"

"Sam is a guy and he's the—"

"Editor for the *Ocean Point Weekly*." Jacob's voice, firm and clipped, cut her off, completing her sentence. "As in Elise's boss."

Madelyn clapped her hands together. "Really? How wonderful. What's he like?"

She worked to keep her voice steady, to not let Jacob's attitude unnerve her. "Sam is great. He's been writing since before I was born. He knows more about journalism than anyone I've ever met and his fiction is amazing. He'll be on the *New York Times* bestseller list one day,

I'm sure of it. But, most of all, he's a good, fair, man."
She inhaled slowly, deliberately, decided to take a gamble
with one more thing. "Jacob, I know you were interested
in journalism when we first met. Sam is a good guy to
get to know if that's still an interest of yours."

It worked. The steeliness in the young man's eyes
softened, his clamped mouth loosened.

Sierra grabbed his forearm. "Oh, Jacob, that's
awesome."

He yanked his arm away, muttered something under
his breath that wasn't audible on Elise's end of the table.
But it didn't need to be. His movements said it all.

So much for the momentary thawing…

She felt sorry for the pretty blonde who looked as if
she'd been struck, her lower lip quivering as she fought the
urge to cry. Maybe *Elise* was the one who shouldn't be
there. Maybe Jacob needed this group more than she did.

"Do the police have anything at all on Ms. Daltry's
murder?" Madelyn took hold of the conversation once
more, obviously determined to keep the discussion on
the subjects of her choosing. "Do they think it's tied to
the robbery of the computer lab?"

Elise swallowed over the lump in her throat, winced
at the way her voice faltered as she spoke. Jacob
unnerved her—there were no two ways about it. "It
looks that way."

The sound of wood scraping against linoleum interrupted further conversation as Sierra jumped up from
the table, her face still crestfallen. "I need to get a refill."

The girl's words were hurried and hushed, her breath hitching between each word.

Elise's heart ached for the young girl who was obviously still smarting from Jacob's public rebuke. If she could only talk to her, make her realize it was *Elise* he was made at, not Sierra. But it didn't take a rocket scientist to know that her presence was a source of stress for Jacob Brown. And by being a source of stress for him, she was one for Sierra as well. Why else would the girl have gotten so spooked when she realized Jacob might catch her and Elise talking?

Elise quietly snapped her cell phone from her waistband and flipped it open in her lap. She needed a Mitchfix, even if it only went one-way.

Hi Mitch.
Thinking about you. Missing you.
Loving you. Can't wait 2 see U.
Yours, Elise.

"Who order spare ribs?" Mia's sweet voice cut through the tension in the room, her slender hands deftly holding a tray that was twice as wide as she was.

Al's hand shot up. "That's mine." His eyes grew wide as saucers as he reached for his plate. "Wow, looks great, Mia. Thank you."

"Taste even better. Who had the Cashew Chicken?" Mia handed the food to Paul upon his grunt. "And pepper steak belong to my Ewise."

Elise reattached the cell phone at her waist and returned Mia's smile. "Thanks, Mia. It looks and smells wonderful."

And it was true. The plate of piping hot comfort food looked and smelled delicious. Unfortunately, she'd lost her appetite, the grumble of hunger in her stomach replaced by the flip-flop of raw nerves.

A warm hand on her shoulder made her pause, thoughts of Jacob and Sierra halted for a brief moment. "I'm sorry that young man has such anger toward you. But you are handling him brilliantly. Keep being your friendly self and I have little doubt you'll win him over."

Elise looked up to see Al's cheerful face looking down at her. "Thanks, Al."

He squeezed her shoulder once more. "Now, can you hand me the salt and pepper?"

She giggled. Al Nedley was both observant and smart. He had a way of diffusing tension in the simplest of ways. A true Godsend at that precise moment.

"Sure." She reached to the center area of the table, grabbed the salt and pepper shaker and handed them up to Al.

Madelyn leaned into her arm as the man returned to his seat, her voice barely a whisper. "So sweet."

Elise pulled back just enough to see the elderly woman's face. "What's sweet?"

The woman looked over the rim of her glasses, her wide, pouty lips turned downward. "Al, that's who. You saw the way he made Janice feel better after class that

first day." Madelyn stole a sideways glance in Al's direction. "But beneath that smile is a card shark the likes
of which New Jersey has never seen. I suppose he got
that way living in a place like Wyoming for so long.
What else is there to do, you know?"

Visions of Madelyn, Al, Janice, and Paul huddled
around a poker table, cigars hanging from their mouths,
was enough to turn Elise's glum mood around. But she
stopped herself short of putting too much thought into
whether or not they played for money or articles of
clothing. There was only so much one could stomach.

While they ate, several of the students shared their
assignments. Some were stilted and wordy, writing as
much a foreign concept to them as math and science
were to her. Others, like Madelyn's friend, Janice,
showed real promise. Madelyn, herself, wrote about a
trip to the candy store as a child, her description written
in much the same way she spoke, exhibiting an almost
breathless quality.

Mia returned to the dining room, her shiny eyes tired
and dull. "It nine o'clock. I close up now?"

Elise looked around the room, surprised to see that
all the other diners had left, including Dean. They'd all
been so absorbed in critiquing each other's work that
three hours had slipped by with barely a notice.

Madelyn made her *tsking* sound. "Oh, we still need
to hear from Al, Paul, Jacob, Sierra, and Elise. I was
looking forward to hearing everybody's. Could you let
us stay a little longer?"

Mia's face dropped a little but recovered quickly, her sunny disposition chasing away all signs of fatigue. "Of course."

Torn between guilt over invading Mia's restaurant beyond closing and not wanting to rock the creative writing class boat more than she already had, Elise shifted in her seat, unsure of what to say.

Fortunately, Al took the ball and ran. "You know what, people? Mia has been most gracious in letting us take this many tables for the past three hours. I don't know about the rest of you, but I'm bushed. I'm just gonna wait on my assignment until class."

A chorus of agreement went around the table, everyone ready to call it a night.

"Sounds great," Elise said, grabbing her coat and bag as she pushed back her chair and stood. "This was really nice, Madelyn, thanks for getting it together. And I really enjoyed everyone's work. Thanks."

"It *was* fun, wasn't it?" Madelyn wrapped her pudgy fingers around the handle of her paisley satchel and slid out of the seat. "I think we need to continue this throughout the class, what do you guys think?"

Surprisingly, everyone nodded. Including Jacob. Maybe there really was hope like Al said…

Elise headed toward the door with Madelyn and Janice, everyone else either just a few steps ahead or a few steps behind. Jacob was at the front of the group, his arm draped protectively over Sierra's shoulder. Elise was surprised to realize just how much she'd enjoyed the evening once they'd gotten through the tension at the beginning. Writing had a tendency to do that in her life and it was neat to see it happen for others too, including Jacob Brown.

"Goodnight, Mia." Elise gave the woman a quick hug as they neared the front door, thrusting a twenty-dollar bill into her apron pocket. "It was great as always."

And it was. Once things had settled down and the critiquing had begun, Elise found herself nibbling on her dinner. A little here, a little there, until her plate was virtually empty.

"You bring Mitch to see me when he back." The woman kissed Elise's forehead before pulling away. "You hear?"

"Yes, Mia."

Al pushed the door open, a burst of cold winter air swirling into the restaurant to the sound of gasps, shivers, and shouting. Shouting?

In an instant, a camera was hoisted onto the shoulder of a large man with dark brown hair and a stubbled face. A woman with perfectly coiffed hair shoved a microphone in Jacob's face as they emerged from the restaurant.

"Jacob Brown?"

Jacob's body tensed, his hand dropping from Sierra's shoulder and pulling into a fist at his side. "Yes?"

The woman pointed to the cameraman who immediately switched to record. She turned back to Jacob, the microphone to her lips.

"Does the recent homicide at Ocean Point Community College bring back painful memories for you and your family?"

The anger that welled inside her at the public humiliation being caused by a fellow journalist was short-lived, the emotion reduced to fear as Jacob Brown turned and looked at her, his eyes filled with a hatred she'd seen just one other time in her life. From his father.

Elise looked away, her eyes drawn to the blonde standing next to him, tears running down the girl's cheeks as she stood hopelessly beside her boyfriend.

EIGHT

SHE WALKED FROM TABLE to table examining each of her stories, making note of their placement and any cuts that needed to be made. The front page story on the completion of Ocean Point Park looked fantastic with its pull-out boxes and accompanying photos.

She had to hand it to Sam, he was a lay-out machine—a veritable composing-room genius.

"You think he'll ever cave and go computer?"

Elise glanced up from page five, her hand grazing Tom's as they reached for the one lone Exacto knife at the same time. "Oh, sorry. You go first." She leaned forward against the table, peeking across to the sports section he was painstakingly moving around. "I don't know if he'll go to a computer layout. The program is kind of expensive from what I hear, and we all know what we're doing this way. No down-time for learning, you know?"

The sports reporter shrugged, the left side of his mouth rising along with his nostril. "Yeah, you're probably right. And I think I catch mistakes better this way."

"Me too. I just noticed a back-to-back 'the' in my zoning meeting story." She looked back down at her own page, her eyes scanning the rest of the article for any additional typos.

"Here, take this one, I think there's a back-up blade in one of these cabinets." Tom handed the blade to Elise and started yanking drawers open, his hand rummaging through each one loudly and quickly. "Yup, here it is."

"Thanks, Tom." She leaned over the mistake and carefully cut the unnecessary word from the page, repositioning the correct one for better spacing.

"Hey, any more trouble from that Brown kid?" Tom paused with the Exacto blade in his hand, his gaze meeting hers across the table. "I heard you say something to Sam yesterday about your critique meeting being kind of tense."

She moved the blade down the article, stopping again in the sixth paragraph to remove an extra *S*. "It was a mess. We met at Mia's to read some of our assignments. You could tell he wasn't happy with my presence, but it didn't really interfere with the work."

"Okay, sounds good. So what happened?" Tom smacked his fist on the front page and raised his hands to his face, letting them slide from his forehead to his chin in exasperation. "I've looked at this story probably *ten* times in the past five minutes and it finally dawns on me that I spelled 'mediate' wrong—duh!"

"I've done that a bunch too. But better to catch it now than when it's staring back at you from the newsstand at

Merv's, right?" Satisfied that page five was clean, she bypassed page six's full-page ad and moved on to seven. "Anyway, when our group was leaving, Joni Goodfellow showed up, her henchman—I mean, cameraman—in tow."

Tom walked over to the composing room computer and sat down. With a click of a few keys, the headline program opened and he retyped mediate in its correct form. "Goodfellow...Goodfellow...oh, wait, I know her. She's the obnoxious chick from Channel 20, right?"

"That's the one." Elise read through the article on Chief Maynard's neighborhood watch program, pleased to see no errors. "She sticks a microphone in Jacob's face as he's walking out of the restaurant. Wants to know if Hannah Daltry's murder is causing issues for his family."

He snickered, his voice dripping with disgust as he ran the corrected headline through the wax machine. "You mean like the issue *she's* raking up by asking that question?"

Tossing the blade into the sill, she walked around the table. "Exactly my point." She pointed at the sports pages he'd yet to proof. "Want an extra pair of eyes?"

"Absolutely, thanks." Tom stuck the new headline on top of the old one, declaring his front page free of errors. Again. "I'm going to take a wild guess here, but I'm betting Goodfellow's question stirred up the guy's anger with you all over again, no?"

"Yup, that about sums it up." She pushed a wayward brown curl off her forehead and slipped her feet from her heels. "But I just don't get why he's so angry at me. His dad was the one who killed all those people. What did I do?"

"You really don't know?" Tom straightened up, his tall, lean form towering above her.

"No. I don't." It was bad enough to know Jacob hated her, but she never took Tom for someone who would project a person's mistakes onto someone else.

He encased her upper arm with his left hand, tipped her chin upward with his right. "It seems to me you are a constant reminder of what his dad did. He's probably not angry at you. But I'm sure he's pissed as all hell at his dad. Unfortunately, since the object of his hatred is dead, he's pushing it onto you—the last one who saw his dad alive. The kid just needs some help."

She felt the moisture on her eyelashes as she shut them tightly. Tom was right. It made all the sense in the world. But knowing it and fixing it were two very different things.

"Hey, I told you…I'm here to help if you need me. Just say the word." Tom's voice, low and gruff, cut through her thoughts, forced her eyes to open and focus on the smoldering grey ones peering back at her intently.

She shivered.

Pulling back, she forced her attention onto the table behind her, her eyes not seeing a single word on the page. If Tom was right, how could she ever change Jacob's anger? And was she imagining it, or was there something in Tom's eyes she'd never noticed before?

"I'll be okay, Tom, thanks." Desperate to diffuse the charged atmosphere in the room, she pointed at his front page. "Um, Tom? You spelled your last name wrong on your top byline."

"What?" Tom leaned over the page, shaking his head almost immediately. "No, I didn't."

"Gotcha."

He reached across, securing her neck gently in the crook of his arm, his free hand rubbing the top of her head. "Better watch it, sugar, or I'll sic Dean on you."

Sugar? Uh oh.

Carefully extracting herself from the sports reporter's grip, she moved down the row of tables to the section's fourth page, anxious to put some distance between them. Maybe teasing wasn't such a good idea.

"Hey, how do you know so much about people?" She scanned the page, stopping to insert a missing period. "Like what you said about Jacob Brown a minute ago."

Tom coughed and leaned over his own page, his face noticeably flushed. "I got a minor in Psychology. People fascinate me. I just wish someone would step up and help this kid out. Like Father Leahy or a school counselor. Before it's too late."

She let his comments roam around in her thoughts, tried parts of them on for size. The Father Leahy comment made sense. Who better to help Jacob channel his anger in the right direction than the senior pastor at St. Theresa's?

"Think you're good with the last few pages of your section?"

"Of course. But why? Where you going?" Tom stopped fiddling with his page and looked up, his brows dipping.

She set the blade down and slipped her feet back into her heels, trying desperately to avoid further eye contact with Tom. The disappointment in his face and stance was unmistakable. The source, though, was in question. Was he simply disappointed she couldn't help with the last three pages? Or was her internal radar pinging for a reason?

"I'm going to give Father Leahy a call. See if maybe he can help." She headed toward the door and stopped. "Thanks, Tom. For listening. It helped more than you can know."

"Any time, Elise. Any time."

She ventured out into the newsroom, her thoughts torn between calling Father Leahy and the vibes she was picking up from Tom. Surely she was crazy. Wasn't she? They'd been working in the same office for nearly a year and she'd never had any indication the sports reporter's feelings were anything other than professional. Until today.

Deep in thought, she rounded the column near the center of the room and smacked into Dean coming from the other direction.

"Whoa, chicky, where are you off to in such a blur?" Dean popped a pretzel into his mouth and held up the snack-size bag. "By the way, thanks for the pretzels."

She rolled her eyes. "Anyone ever taught you about office etiquette?"

He raised the bag toward the ceiling and emptied the remaining contents straight into his mouth. "Office eti-what?"

"Office eti-*quette*. You know, stuff like not rummaging through other people's drawers and stuff?"

Dean swallowed his mouthful of pretzels and exhaled through closed lips. "Etiquette, schmetiquette. I'd miss out on perfectly good snacks if I listened to that crap. What do you think I am, stupid? Sheesh."

Shaking her head with mock irritation, she pushed past the photographer and headed toward her desk.

"Wait! Could you maybe think about getting some crackers or something? The pretzels are getting a little boring."

She turned and cast her best impression of an evil eye in his direction.

He laughed. "Sweetheart, you couldn't be a shrew if you tried. So save the effort and just rotate the snacks a little, okay?"

"Yeah, yeah, whatever. I've got work to do." She dropped into her chair and reached for the phone, retracting her hand as a thought skirted through her mind. "Hey, Dean?"

The wiry twenty-something retraced his steps, stopping at her desk. "You find a Chip Ahoy! or somethin'?"

Elise waved her hand in the air, her mind rewinding

to Wednesday evening. "No. But I was wondering how you know Sierra McDermott?"

He crumbled the empty pretzel bag and sent it sailing in the direction of Debbie's desk. "I don't. Who is she? Is she hot?"

She swiveled around in her chair, cocked an eyebrow in the photographer's direction. "Wait. You can commandeer pretzels from my desk without asking, yet you'll play coy when I ask you a simple question? I see how this works." She reached across her arm and retrieved a pen from her desktop, tapping it on her leg.

"See how *what* works? I have no idea who you're talking about." Dean blew outward, a strand of blond hair floating upward.

"Oh, please." She pulled off her left heel and rubbed her ankle, a blister forming where the back strap met her skin. "Do you usually sit so close to women you don't know? Wait, don't answer that. I really don't want to know."

Crossing his arms across his old, beat-up Grateful Dead t-shirt, he leaned against the pole. "You're kinda cute when you're babbling, you know that?"

She held up her hands, palms outward. "No, no, no, no, no. Don't you dare start too."

"*Too?*" Dean's mouth curved into his trademark devil-grin. "Someone sniffing around Mitch's girl?"

Ugh.

"No! Just answer the question. How do you know Sierra?" She turned her palms inward, rubbed her eyes with the heels of her hands as she waited for a response from the King of Rhetoric.

"I don't know a Sierra. Why do you think I do?" He reached around her body and yanked open her top left drawer. "Any treats in *here*?"

She smacked his hand off the handle and threw her body against the drawer. "I think you *do* because you were sitting in Mia's with her Wednesday night, hunched over a computer…which brings me to question number two. Why on earth were you messing with a computer?"

Dean pushed off the pole, his sickly white skin sporting an unusual red hue across his cheeks. "Oh. Her. *Please*. Not my type. Not even close. I was just having a hard time figuring out how to turn the damn computer on. She stuck around for a few extra minutes to help. Shows how intense the interaction was when I couldn't tell you if her name was Sierra or Trixy. Though, if it was Trixy, I'd 'uv remembered. Buh-lieve you, me."

Men.

"But wait. Why do *you* need a computer?" She stood and followed him down the hallway toward his darkroom. "You despise them, remember?"

Dean stepped into his darkroom and pointed at the 'Do Not Disturb' sign hanging on the door. "There are some things I want to be able to see, and apparently a computer makes that easier to access."

She felt her face begin to warm, the meaning behind his words hitting her between the eyeballs. Grrrreeeeeaaaatttttt….

"Look, missy, don't ask a question you don't want me to answer." Dean pulled his camera bag from his shoulder and stuck it on the table in the center of his small room. "I would've thought you'd have learned that by now."

Nodding, and feeling more than a little foolish, she turned back towards her desk.

"And Elise? That's Chips…A…Hoy. Blue package."

NINE

8:15 p.m.

MITCH BURNS PULLED the strap of his carry-on further up his shoulder, his stride quickening as the security check-point came into view. As much as he'd enjoyed working with Jonathan and the high school kids, he couldn't wait to see Elise. To hold her in his arms again. God, how he'd missed that…

He caught his reflection in the glass partition of an airport restaurant as he walked down the brown carpeted corridor, his hair surprisingly okay after sleeping on a plane for two hours. Good. He wanted it ready for her fingers to run through.

The second he rounded the x-ray machines, he saw her, his heart rate picking up speed as their eyes met across the waiting area. She was every bit as beautiful as he remembered—her slender body clad in form-fitting tan slacks and a soft white v-neck sweater, her brown curls spilling halfway down her back. But it was her smile he'd missed the most. The way it lit up her eyes when they spent time together…like now.

He crossed the distance between them in seconds,

dropping his bag at his feet and pulling her into his arms, her subtle perfume and shampoo mingling together perfectly. "Oh, 'Lise, I've missed you so much." He reveled in the feel of her body, the warmth of her breath against his neck.

They stood that way for a long time. Completely oblivious to the waves of passengers heading to and from their planes. This was the way it was supposed to be. The two of them—together. Always.

Her mouth moved against his skin but the throng of passengers and well-wishers made it difficult to hear her words. Reluctantly he released her, his hand cupping her chin and raising it upward. "I didn't hear what you said."

He saw her swallow, caught the dampness in her eyes as she spoke. "I missed you so much, Mitch."

Lowering his mouth to hers, he kissed her, her lips soft and warm against his own. He could sense people slowing down to gawk, but it didn't matter. He was exactly where he wanted to be. People or no people.

After a long moment, she stepped back, rubbed his arm with her hand. "How was your flight?"

"Great. I slept the entire time." He could hear the gruffness to his voice as he contemplated another kiss. "Today was one-on-one evaluations with the kids and we started pretty early."

"*Luggage from Tran-Air flight fifty-five eighty is now arriving on carousel four.*"

Elise pointed upward at a ceiling speaker, her eyes sparkling. "It's official. You're here to stay. Let's get your stuff. You can nap in the car on the way home if you're still tired."

Grabbing his carry-on, he fell into step with her as they rounded the corner toward baggage claim. "I'm not tired anymore."

"Good." She grinned, her soft hand intertwining with his as they walked. "Because I think all my talking would keep you awake."

He laughed. "You? Never."

"Hey!"

It felt good to be back home, to be teasing and laughing with one another. It was funny how life could change in such a short period of time. A year ago, he was content to spend his non-working hours behind his desk at the department. Pushing paper and planning training programs. Now he wanted every waking hour to be spent with her. It didn't matter what they did, just so long as they were together.

"So how was work today? Anything exciting?"

"Sure, if you call proofing copy exciting." Her laughed echoed through the corridor as they rounded the corner toward Baggage Claim Four. "Other than that, it was a fairly mundane day. Confusing, but mundane."

"Confusing? How so?" He grabbed his black suitcase from the conveyer belt and guided her toward the short-term parking door. "Dean acting normal or something?"

"Dean will never be normal. But, yeah, he was one of the confusing parts." She motioned to the third row of cars. "I'm over there, see?"

He took the keys from her hand, popped the trunk, and tossed his bags inside before walking around to the passenger side and opening the door for Elise. When she slid into her seat, he leaned over and kissed her on the lips. "God, I'm glad I'm back."

She smiled up at him. "So am I. You have no idea."

The drive to Ocean Point took about two hours and four toll booths. They talked almost non-stop. He about the camp and Jonathan, she about work and her critique group. She seemed happy, talkative, yet he couldn't shake the feeling that something was weighing on her. He waited, hoped she'd spill it on her own, but when she didn't he asked point blank.

"You okay, baby? There's something in your voice tonight that seems a little off. Something happen while I was gone? You worried about this murder?" He slid his right hand across the center console and pulled her hand into his. "About the fact that the guy hasn't been caught yet? Because I'll keep you safe, you know that."

She sighed softly and leaned her head against the seat. "I know. It's just…" Her voice trailed off as she turned and looked out the window, her free hand fidgeting with a piece of lint on her slacks.

"Hey." He let go of her hand and turned her face, taking his eyes off the road to meet hers in snatches. "It's just *what*?"

"Jacob."

"Huh?"

She raised her hands to her face, her fingers trembling ever so slightly. "Jacob Brown."

He glanced at the road ahead, then pulled his gaze back inside the car and onto Elise's troubled face. "The mayor's kid? What about him?"

"He was in my writing class over the weekend and at that critique meeting I told you about Wednesday night." Elise shifted in her seat, clasping her hands in her lap.

He remembered Wednesday night. She'd seemed distracted during their call, her voice breaking a few times throughout the conversation. When he'd asked if she was okay, she'd chalked it up to being tired. Claimed it had been a long day tracking down facts about the murdered teacher.

It hadn't rung true at the time—his instincts telling him there was something troubling her that went way beyond lack of sleep. But he'd let it go, knowing they both had to get up early in the morning. Now he wished he'd pushed. It was obvious that something had happened.

"He giving you a hard time?"

She exhaled slowly, deliberately, as if she was trying to find the courage to speak. It scared him.

"He's angry."

"At you?" He tightened his grip on the steering wheel, his gaze alternating between the road ahead and the woman beside him.

"It seems that way. It was just looks on Saturday. Looks and demeanor. He made a sarcastic comment during class that was aimed at me, but, other than that, nothing." Her voice grew softer as she continued, causing him to strain to pick out her words. "Then during the critique meeting I thought there was a chance he might soften. It didn't last long, but it was there. That is until Joni Goodfellow stirred it all up again."

He racked his brain for a face to match the name Elise had said. Joni Goodfellow..."Wait, that's the Channel 20 beat reporter, right? What sewer is she climbing around in now?"

Elise turned her face back toward the window, her quiet words taking on a shaky quality. "She showed up outside Mia's. Stuck a microphone in Jacob's face. Asked him if the Hannah Daltry murder was bringing back bad memories for his family."

"You can't be serious." He glanced across at his fiancée, his heart breaking at the uncharacteristic slant to her mouth. "Don't answer that. I've seen the woman in action with my own two eyes. So what happened?"

"Let's just say if looks could kill, I wouldn't be sitting here right now." She unclasped her hands and turned them upward. "I don't know what to do. Tom thinks he's just projecting his anger for his father onto me. And maybe he's right. But even if he is, what can I do about it? I don't think this kid's anger will amount to anything besides a few dirty looks and an icy comment here and there...but I don't know."

"It better not." As soon as he heard the tone of his voice, he rushed to soften it, reluctant to give Elise any indication that he was concerned about the situation. A young man, mourning the unexpected death of his father after a string of horrific crimes, was showing anger toward the woman who brought his father down. Sure, it could be a simple case of projection like the sports reporter said. But there was also a very good chance it could turn into more.

He pulled his hand from the steering wheel and traced a line down her jaw with his index finger, savoring the feel of her skin. She'd been through too much over the past year. Hell would freeze over before he'd see her go through something like that ever again.

"Anyone witness his attitude toward you?" He willed his voice to sound relaxed. "You know…anyone ask what was up?"

She nodded. "He's not shy about his feelings regardless of who's in the room. In fact, he turned a little of it onto Ms. Daltry Saturday when she called him on his attitude."

"Really?" He'd been listening all evening, hearing every word she said. But suddenly a different part of his brain was processing. "What happened?"

"Ms. Daltry commented on his anger, kind of embarrassed him in front of the class. Which, of course, earned her an evil eye and a hefty dose of attitude also. It was so blatant, even one of the older guys in my class commented on it." Elise scooted to the left, gently resting her head on his upper arm. She smelled good. Sweet.

They fell into a comfortable silence as he exited the parkway and headed south. Her breathing was soft and measured against his arm as his thoughts bounced between the woman against him and the things she'd shared about Jacob Brown and the murder victim.

Could her death be more than just a casualty of another crime? It certainly warranted a little checking around. Just to see where it might lead.

He turned onto Second Street when he reached Ocean Point, her car seeming to know the way with very little guidance from him. He couldn't wait to be alone in her apartment, just to hold her for as long as he wanted—no baggage announcements or curious strangers to worry about.

"You think I can read your assignment for class?"

She pulled her head off his arm and smiled shyly, her eyes casting downward briefly. "Sure. Eventually."

"Eventually? What's with the eventually stuff?" Mitch pulled into an empty space outside her apartment building and stepped out of the car, crossing around the hood to her door. He opened it and offered his hand, enjoying the feel of her long, thin fingers intertwined with his.

"I wrote a scene about you. About how you've impacted my life. I don't want you to see it until it's perfect. Like you." She stepped into his outstretched arms and let out a quiet little noise. A happy noise as he liked to call it.

"Awwww, baby. I've missed you." He held her tight, his lips brushing against her hair, her forehead. "But isn't this thing due tomorrow morning?"

"Yes. I just want to hold off showing you for a little

while longer, okay?" She rocked with him as he gently swayed from side to side, the cold April air barely registering on his skin. "You should see what Ms. Daltry wrote as an example. It was so powerful. So engaging. I'm not sure my writing will ever be as strong as hers."

He let go of her shoulders and stepped back, spreading his arms outward. "How can you say that when you're writing about *moi*?"

Her sweet laugh lifted his heart. He placed his hand on the small of her back and guided her upstairs to her apartment. "What? You laugh?"

"You're funny, that's all. I'm not saying my subject matter isn't incredible and worthy of fabulous writing. I'm just saying I'm not sure I'll ever be the writer that woman is—I mean—*was*."

He massaged her shoulder as they walked up the steps. "I have little doubt you'll be famous one day. You are an amazing writer, Elise Jenkins." And he meant it. But even more than her ability to write, he admired the class with which she pursued each and every story. Joni Goodfellow could certainly stand to learn a few things from Elise.

"Thank you." Tiny points of red spread across her cheeks as she looked back at him, her humility yet another of the many endearing qualities he loved about this woman. Elise Jenkins was the least boastful person he'd ever met. And her empathy for others? Wow. It never ceased to blow him away every time he was lucky enough to witness her interaction with another person.

As his Aunt Betty said…he'd done good. Real good.

TEN

IT WAS HARD NOT TO LOOK at the desk where Hannah Daltry had been murdered. Hard not to imagine the fear that had raced through the woman's heart when she realized she was in the wrong place at the wrong time—again.

The O.P.P.D. had cleared the classroom by Friday morning, confident they had whatever evidence there was to be found. But still, there was something unsettling about sitting a few feet from the exact spot where a woman had been murdered.

Elise would have thought she'd be used to it by now. Lord knew she'd been through more than her fair share of murder investigations, stood in more crime scenes than she'd ever imagined. Yet it didn't get any easier. And she doubted it ever would.

"Feels weird to be here, doesn't it?"

Elise looked up, her thoughts interrupted by a soft spoken voice that seemed as hesitant and nervous as it did young. Sierra McDermott stood beside Elise's desk, her hands anxiously clenching and unclenching at her sides.

The girl cast a nervous glance at the door, shifted foot to foot. "I just wanted to tell you that I know you had nothing to do with that reporter hounding Jacob the other night. I've read your stuff. You've got more class than that."

Not sure of what to say or how to react, Elise willed her voice to remain calm. "Wow. You have no idea how much it helps to hear you say that. I feel just awful for Jacob. For what's he's been through and for what he's still going through."

Sierra nodded, her eyes trained on the doorway, her head cocked to the side as if she was listening for something no one else could hear. "All I wanted was for the media to stop talking about his dad. To focus on something new. But now it's even w—"

The girl leapt forward as if she'd been stabbed, her body moving through the maze of desks like a running back in search of the end zone. Elise felt her mouth drop open as Sierra slid into her seat just moments before Jacob entered the room.

How on earth?

It was a rhetorical question, really, because she knew the answer. It was called *love* and Sierra's reaction wasn't anything different than she could probably do with Mitch. Call it a sixth sense, a feeling. When you loved someone with your entire being, you could sense their presence, their mood from a hundred paces away.

Sierra was smart enough to hear Jacob in the hallway

and perceptive enough to know he'd not take kindly to her spending time in enemy camp.

Sighing, Elise reached into her backpack and extracted her assignment folder and a pen. She was looking forward to Sam teaching the class, she really was. But in the matter of twenty short minutes, Ms. Daltry had struck a chord inside her head. Then again, how much of that was Ms. Daltry herself and how much was simply the power of her work and the hold it seemed to take on Elise's heart?

"Good morning, class, my name is Sam Hughes. I'll be taking over for the late Hannah Daltry." The balding man walked into the class, setting a new black briefcase on the front table. "Is everyone here this morning?"

Elise looked around at her classmates, recognizing many of the faces from the critique session Wednesday night. But where were Madelyn and her crew? She swung her head to the right, searched the other side of the room, fairly certain she would have noticed the elderly contingent when she walked in. Nope, not there.

She raised her hand, grinning at Sam from her desk. "I think we're missing four."

A series of hurried footsteps outside the door picked up speed; several hushed voices drowned out periodically by a louder, busier one.

Madelyn.

Sure enough, Madelyn Conner breezed into the classroom, her eyes wide, her face contorted. "Please excuse us, sir. *One* of us was being a bit anal about our parking spot this morning."

Anal?

Elise laughed. Sam bit back his own smile, his hand reaching outward. "You must be Madelyn Conner, am I right?" He grasped Madelyn's hand as he spoke, the threesome still standing in the doorway. "No explanation needed. We're all late from time to time. Even when we aren't picky about where we put our car."

"You tell her." Al smacked Sam on the back as he walked to his seat, his Yankees cap firmly in place on his head. Dropping into the seat in front of Elise, he turned around and rolled his eyes. "Any chance you've got a flask handy? That woman will be the death of me yet. You wait and see."

It took everything in her power not to laugh out loud, to tip off the conversation to the woman taking up shop in the seat next to hers. She waved a greeting at Madelyn, hoped the gesture would enable her mouth to remain closed and unable to laugh. It worked, until she looked back at Sam and saw his lips twitching.

Aye yi yi.

"Anyway, I'd like to welcome you all to class this morning and express my deepest sympathies on the death of Hannah Daltry. The two of us were in a critique group together that met every Sunday. In fact, I was just with her the day before she was found. She was an amazingly talented writer and a truly sweet woman. She will be missed." Sam leaned against the table and looked around at the faces assembled in front of him. "Is it safe to assume that most of you in this class are here because you have a genuine interest in writing?"

Heads nodded.

"Good. That'll make teaching this group even more fun. For me, there's nothing better than working with creative minds. You never know what's going to happen next or where a brainstorming session or writing assignment will take you." He stood up, wandered down the aisles. "I understand you were given an assignment by Ms. Daltry to write a one-page scene that conveys emotion, sucks the reader into your world. Is that correct?"

Again, heads nodded.

"Great. Let's get started. Who'd like to read first?"

Madelyn's hand shot into the air, her plump body shifting in her seat.

"Madelyn? You ready to go?" Sam stopped and pointed to the woman beside Elise.

"I am. But I'd like to volunteer Al."

Elise choked back a laugh as Al raised his hand to his neck and pulled upward, simulating a noose.

"Al?" Sam folded his arms across his chest and waited, obviously as amused by the senior set as the rest of the class. "Any chance you'd like to go first?"

"Do I have a choice?" Al plucked his cap from his head and set it on his desk, his left hand rummaging around in his bag. He plucked out his assignment sheet, wrinkled and soiled, and looked up at Sam. "Do I stand? Sit? Jump?"

Sam's lips twitched again. "Why don't you go ahead and stand so we can see you. Besides, when you're all published you have to be able to speak in front of a group. So we might as well get some practice in that area as well."

Al made his way up to the front of the room, his stocky frame reminiscent of a big old teddy bear. One that just happened to have a sidekick named Madelyn. He stopped beside the table, his left fist resting on the top as his right hand held the paper.

"Big Bird told me not to do it. Ace, the talking fire dog, told me not to do it. My mom told me not to do it. Even my Uncle Zeb, who rarely said two words, told me not to do it.

But it didn't matter. Not at that very moment, with Cedrick's big face staring down at me.

Cedrick was one of the cool kids. The ones everyone wants to be friends with. Why? We don't know. And we don't care. We just want their acknowledgement, their acceptance. We're not yet old enough, or wise enough, to realize their acknowledgement is fleeting, insincere. We're too inexperienced to know they're not the kind of friends you want.

In the grand scheme of things, what was the big deal over lighting a small match, seeing how long I could hold it before I had to shake it out? Cedrick was watching. That's all that mattered.

It was my chance to show I wasn't a coward. My chance to be a big shot too.

So I lit that match. And I held that match until I couldn't hold it for another second, tossing it onto the floor, my eyes intent on Cedrick's face. Where was the approval? Where was the admiration? Where was my invitation to the cool kid club?

It was in the exact same place Cedrick was when I burned my arm trying to put out the fire I had caused. It was in the exact same place Cedrick was when the doctors tried to fix my arm with one painful procedure after the other. It was in the exact same place Cedrick was when the bills poured in, one after the other.

It, like Cedrick, was nowhere to be found."

The room was quiet for a moment as everyone took in Al's work, tried unsuccessfully not to look at his left wrist.

"Excellent, Al. Very nice." Sam walked up the side aisle and stopped beside the man. "Tell me the emotion this piece evoked in you. Anyone?"

"Humiliation. Regret."

Elise looked over her shoulder, her gaze falling on Jacob as he shifted in his seat, pulling his arm back down.

"Excellent, Mr...."

"Jacob is fine."

If Sam realized who Jacob was, he didn't miss a beat, his hands clapping together quickly. "Nicely done, Jacob." He turned to Al. "That's what you were going for, right?"

Al nodded, held his left hand outward. "Absolutely. What other emotion could there be after such a stupid move?"

"Did it take you a long time to get over that emotion?" Jacob's voice, low and shaky, emerged from the back of the room.

"Not sure you ever do. That kind of stuff has a weird domino effect. Throughout your life…in all you think and do."

Sam patted Al's shoulder and turned back to the class. "Thank you, Al. Okay, Miss?" He pointed behind Elise, his face encouraging.

"Sierra. Sierra McDermott."

"Sierra. Would you like to go next?"

"I guess…" The petite blonde grabbed her paper and headed up the aisle, her free hand jammed in her jeans pocket. When she reached the front of the room, she dropped her head down and shifted from foot to foot. She started to read, stopped, coughed, and began again, her nervousness obvious to all.

"It was not what it seemed.

But how could he tell?

All he'd meant to do was help. To make things better.

Yet somehow it went horribly wrong. What was supposed to be better was now worse. What was supposed to help, hurt more.

He cowered in a corner, alone, eyeing his

mistakes from afar. Desperate to fix things, unsure of how—or if—it could be done.

Seeking help would bring an end. Ignoring it could bring a loss much greater and provide an unjust freedom.

It was not what it seemed.

But how could he tell?"

Elise cocked her head to the side as she considered Sierra's piece. Despite the hurried read-through and the wooden voice with which it was spoken, it was still thought-provoking and ripe with emotion.

"Nicely written, Sierra." Sam walked down the center aisle, stopping midway and turning around. "Who would like to comment?"

Madelyn raised her hand, beamed when Sam sought her opinion. "Desperation. Confusion."

Sam nodded. "I think there's more, though that's good." He pointed at Paul, who surprisingly had raised his hand.

"Fear."

"Yes!" Sam turned back to Sierra, and winked. "Thank you, Sierra. I'd love to see you expound even more. Make it a little longer, building on the emotion, digging even deeper."

Sierra smiled shyly and practically ran back to her seat. Elise looked over her shoulder at the girl, hoping to meet her eye, to offer a complimentary smile. But Jacob was there, patting her arm, saying something only Sierra could hear.

"Who's ready to go next?" The room grew eerily quiet as Sam waited for a volunteer. Feeling his gaze, she looked up shyly and shrugged. Why not? She had to read it at some point, right?

"Elise, why don't you c'mon up and—"

"I'll go." Jacob's chair lurched backward as he jumped to his feet.

"Okay, Jacob, thank you." Sam stepped to the side of the room, crossed his arms, and leaned against the door frame, his facial muscles relaxed despite the slight furrow to his brow.

Elise straightened her shoulders and fiddled with her pen, unsure of whether she should look at Jacob as he read or focus on something else like the clock above his head.

The young man cleared his throat a few times, his hand slightly trembling as he looked past Elise and offered a half-smile.

Sierra.

She was glad to know he had someone in his life who gave him courage. Someone who made him smile. Sierra McDermott, although shy and nervous, seemed to be a sweet girl. And she was head-over-heels in love with Jacob Brown.

"I see the face peering back—familiar, yet different. Features I know, a person I don't.

The eyes are still blue like the sky up above. The nose still long and straight and a little bit crooked. The mouth still ready to spread in a smile...

Yet the picture they create when they come together will be changed in my heart forever.

I study it daily looking for clues. Was that sparkle I saw a glint all along? That smile I treasured a clever disguise?

I try to make their facts mesh with mine. To pinpoint the moment his path turned wrong.

But as the days go by and the hurt remains, I fear their image will win in the end.

It's not that I don't know it's there; it's just that I want someone to care. He was a monster for a moment, my dad for a lifetime."

Jacob's piece was met with absolute silence, save a few bodies shifting uncomfortably in their seats. Elise looked quickly at her hands, then back up at the young man whose voice shook along with his paper.

It was brilliant. Poignant. Thought provoking. And it made his attitude toward her understandable. Although his father had done awful things, she could see how Jacob might view her as the moment his idyllic world changed. The moment all the bad things became fact and his perception of his father became wrong.

But what Jacob needed to realize, to come to peace with, was the fact that his perception wasn't wrong. His image of his father—the man he knew—was real too.

Sam's voice cut through her thoughts as he began to clap. Quietly at first, then louder and louder as more hands joined in. "Young man, you have no idea how much your words could teach people. Make them see things from another perspective. Thank you. For making us all think."

Jacob's face lowered, his Adam's apple pronounced as he swallowed. When he glanced up again, his eyes were moist, his mouth showing signs of a tentative, yet genuine, smile. "I wish more people would think."

Her boss's head nodded as he pushed off the door frame and addressed the class. "Okay, I think it's fairly obvious, but who would like to give me the emotions they felt while listening to this piece…the emotions the writer was feeling, trying to convey."

Janice raised her hand. "Despair over the loss of something innocent, and, I think, resignation as well."

"Good." Sam turned back to Jacob. "Jacob, if there ever comes a time you'd like to share that with the paper, I'd be honored to publish it. If it makes even *one* person think, then it did its job."

Elise watched as Jacob's eyes widened in surprise, his cheeks reddened with embarrassment, his smile lifted with hope. And at that very moment, as Jacob Brown's writing was being publicly validated and his feelings acknowledged, she was reminded—once again—why she loved and respected Sam Hughes.

ELEVEN

9:30 a.m.

HE RESTED HIS CHIN on tented fingers and stared unseeingly at the white board on the far wall of his office for the umpteenth time that morning.

The red "x" in the upper left corner represented Ocean Point Gifts. The first of the three robberies. The suspect had gotten away with a handful of beachy Christmas ornaments and a stack of postcards.

The "x" in the bottom left corner was Merv's. Hit up two weeks ago, the neighborhood pharmacy was light a few pairs of cheap sunglasses and a couple of inexpensive watches.

The third and most recent "x" was dead-center. It denoted the two laptops stolen from the mobile computer lab at Ocean Point Community College and the resulting murder of Hannah Daltry.

The first two robberies had followed a distinct pattern. Both took place on a Sunday night when the shops were closed and night-time traffic was at a minimum. In both instances, there were no signs of forced entry, yet all employees had been questioned and cleared of suspicion. Both were minor hits, nothing of significant monetary value missing.

Although the third location had been unlocked to begin with, the robbery itself followed the same basic pattern as the first two. Sunday evening. Campus was quiet. Sure, computers were a bigger take in the grand scheme of things…but, in a roomful of thirty, two constituted a minor hit.

"You just can't stay away, can you, Detective?"

Mitch Burns glanced at the door and grinned at the head peeking around the corner. "Hey, Chief. What are you doing here on a Saturday?"

Kevin Maynard pushed the door open a few extra inches and walked across the room to Mitch's desk. "I called in a little while ago to check on things and Mindy said you were here working."

"And you couldn't wait to see me, could you?" Mitch dropped his legs to the ground and stood, shaking his boss's hand.

"You could say that." Chief Maynard sat down in the empty chair across from Mitch. "When'd you get in?"

"A little after eight last night. 'Lise picked me up and we went back to her place for a while. Didn't get home until about two this morning." Mitch motioned to the unopened Coke can on his desk, then handed it to his boss. "It's good to be home."

Chief Maynard popped his can open and took a long, slow, deliberate pull. "We gotta get this case wrapped up, Mitch. The stakes have gotten too high."

He should have known the chief wouldn't show his face on a weekend for a social call. But the man was right. The murder of Hannah Daltry brought the rash of seemingly petty robberies to a whole new level.

Mitch set down his own drink and stood, covered the distance between his desk and the white board in four long strides. "That's what I've been working on all morning."

"And?"

"I've got a few thoughts, just not sure how much weight to put on them at this point." Mitch pointed to the "x" denoting Ocean Point Gifts. "Granted there's not a whole lot of valuable things in the gift shop, but I know Gerty's got some china teapots from Ireland in there that are worth a heck of a lot more than some postcards and Christmas ornaments."

The boss nodded and sat back, his eyes taking on the squinty look he got while absorbing a situation. "Go on."

Mitch pointed to the "x" for Merv's. "If this thief was a pro, we'd be dealing with missing narcotics…not purple sunglasses and a cheap-o watch or two."

Without waiting for his boss to comment, Mitch continued, his gut playing out loud for the first time all morning. "And then we've got the computer lab here," he pointed at the big red "x" in the center of the board, "which only lost two laptops out of thirty. Almost as if they were token takes, you know?"

He glanced over at the chief, noticed the slow nod to the man's head as he listened.

"The one thing I've been coming back to all morning long is this—I think the robberies are finished."

"You think he's going to move on to another town?" Chief Maynard glanced down at the cell phone attached to his waist, pushed a button on its left side, then looked back at Mitch for an answer to his question.

"No. I don't think he's going to move on. I think he's done. That murder was the last thing he intended. He got caught in a small-play game and simply got scared."

His boss stood and retraced his steps back toward Mitch's door. "That was Denise just now. If I don't get home, I'm not gonna be a real popular guy this weekend. I'll leave you to your work. Sounds like you've got something here."

Mitch walked over to the door with his boss. "I think so, too."

Chief Maynard stopped in the doorway and turned, his good-buddy persona quickly overshadowed by his top-cop tone. "Finish this up, Mitch. I'm counting on you."

"Yes, sir."

He stood there, staring into the hallway for a few moments, his mind playing through everything he'd just gone over with the chief. But it was the nagging part he'd neglected to tell the man that commanded most of his attention.

Wandering back to his desk, he sat down, pulled the coroner's report from the manila envelope on his desk and stared at the cause of death for the third time that morning. Strangulation. Bruising on the victim's body pointed to hands as the murder weapon. Suspected time of death, based on condition of the body and temperature, was approximated to have been Sunday evening between seven and ten.

The reports written by the responding officer noted all the pertinent facts. Condition of body: full rigor. Suspected entry point: classroom doorway. Suspected position of assailant: behind. Approximate age of victim: early forties. Hair color: brown.

The write-up was thorough, all the information legible and understandable. But written reports, regardless of their quality, were a poor substitute for a visual of the crime scene.

He pressed the intercom button on the bottom of his desk phone and waited.

"Yes, Detective Burns?"

"Mindy, do you know if Sorelli's around today?"

"I think he is. Should I tell him you want to see him?"

He looked down at the crime scene write-up, his eyes focused on the assailant's position. "Yeah, I'd like to talk to him ASAP."

Mitch leaned back in his chair and ran a hand through his hair, waiting. He hadn't meant to spend so much time there on a Saturday, but he couldn't leave. Not yet, anyway.

A rapid knock at his door announced Sorelli's arrival.

"You wanted to see me, Mitch?"

"Yeah, c'mon in."

The department's patrolman and star photographer pushed open the door and strolled into Mitch's office, his large, basketball-sized head seeming to spring from his shoulders rather than a neck. "When'd you get back?"

"Last night." Mitch shook the officer's hand and nodded at the vacant chair across from his desk. "Been wading through the reports on the Daltry murder investigation."

Sorelli's mouth spread upward on the right side. "Figured you'd be at it the second you got back. Screwy, ain't it?"

Mitch interlaced his fingers in mid-air and rested the back of his head in his palms. "Screwy, how so?"

Sorelli pulled a toothpick from his back pocket and started picking at his teeth. "This used to be such a quiet town, you know? Then we had all those murders last summer. Thought it was the last we'd see of that kind of thing for a long time. Apparently I was wrong."

Nodding, Mitch considered Sorelli's words. The man was right. Ocean Point was no longer the sleepy little town it once was. The murders last summer had been a first for him as a detective. Yet here he was again, less than a year later, investigating another murder…before talk of the first case had even died down.

"You took pictures, right?"

The toothpick paused. "Of the crime scene? Of course."

"I want to see 'em." Mitch dropped his hands to the desk and lifted the write-up. "Kurdle did a great job on these reports. But you and I both know that the visual is where it's at."

Sorelli tossed his toothpick into the wastebasket beside Mitch's desk and stood. "Give me five."

"Thanks, Sorelli."

While he waited to see the pictures, he made some notes on a pad of paper. Thoughts and impressions of everything he'd seen so far, including the things he'd shared with the chief.

But it was the part he didn't write down that troubled him most. He didn't need the written word to bring it home. It was already there, eating at his subconscious. After all, how could anyone ignore their own part in another person's death?

TWELVE

6:20 p.m.

SHE SNUGGLED CLOSER, listening to the rhythmic beating of his heart against her ear. It was a peaceful, calming sound at the end of a long day, yet she knew him well enough to know that he was troubled by something.

Elise snatched the remote from the coffee table and looked up at Mitch.

"Do you mind if I shut this off?" It was a rhetorical question more than anything else since his gaze was fixed on the wall, his thoughts obviously somewhere other than the sitcom on the screen.

"Huh? What?" He pulled his focus off faraway places long enough to bend his head and steal a quick kiss. "Sure, whatever you want, 'Lise."

She giggled. "You have absolutely no idea what I just asked you, do you?"

"Sure I do," he said, shaking his head at the same time.

"I didn't think so." Elise dropped her legs to the ground and sat up.

"Whoa, where are you going?"

"Nowhere. Just want to see your face a little

easier." She spun her legs toward him, then pulled them up and under her, resting her left elbow on the back of the couch. "Are you okay, sweetie? You were kinda quiet during dinner, and just now…you were a million miles away."

He ran his hand across his face and through his hair. "I'm sorry. I didn't realize…"

Reaching outward, she cupped the side of his face in her right hand. "Hey, I'm not looking for an apology. Just want to know if there's anything I can do."

He pulled his legs from under the coffee table and turned his body slightly to the right. "I guess my mind is back at the office. And I'm sorry about that. If I'd realized just how much this was gonna bug me I wouldn't have come."

She held her index finger to his lips to silence his apology. "Hey. I'm glad you came. I like being with you no matter what. Please know that. Always."

He reached out, wrapped one of her curls around his finger and simply looked at her, the love in his eyes making the butterfly brigade in her stomach take flight.

Elise closed her eyes, reveled in the feel of his soft hand as it left her hair and moved down her face, stopping beside her chin as his lips met hers. The kiss lasted several long minutes, the beat of her heart accelerating rapidly beneath her hunter green sweater.

When they stopped, she opened her eyes and smiled. "I love you, Mitch."

"I love you, 'Lise." His voice was gruff and raspy, the

longing in his eyes raw as he leaned his head into the couch. "Nothing like pushing work out of my mind, huh?"

"But it's back now, isn't it?" She wished she could wipe away the worry from his face, keep the aura of the past few seconds front and center in his life. But that wasn't reality and she knew it. He was a great detective because he cared about the people he served. Change that and he wouldn't be the man she loved.

He nodded. "Yeah."

"Can I help? You know that anything you say stays between us."

Mitch pushed off the couch and walked over to the lone window in the tiny living room. "I know that. It's just…" he pulled the curtains back and looked outside, his body tense and rigid. "Awww, 'Lise this Hannah Daltry investigation is weighing on me on a whole different level."

"How's that?" She debated going over to him, wrapping her arms around his waist as he stared out the window, but she didn't. There were times when space was best.

"Last summer I was racing to figure out who the killer was so I could keep others from falling prey. But this time I can't help but feel I'm responsible."

She gasped. "How? Why?" Her heart thudded against her chest as she waited for him to explain his words.

"Think about it, 'Lise. If I'd taken the first two robberies more seriously, acted quicker, your teacher would still be alive."

"Oh, Mitch, no!" She jumped off the couch and

walked over to him, held his face in her hands. "You can't think like that. Not ever. You were investigating those robberies. You were doing your job. This was not your fault, Mitch Burns."

His arms encircled her shoulders and pulled her close, the tension in his body subsiding. When he finally spoke, his voice was quiet, emotional. "Baby, I love you."

"I love you too." She took his hand in hers and tugged him toward the couch. "Come on back and sit with me."

"You sit. I'm okay." He squeezed her hand, then released it. "I'm too keyed up to sit."

"O-kay…" Elise wandered back to the couch. "So what are you thinking about all of this now that you've had a chance to look at the evidence?"

Mitch shrugged. "I don't know. But I did think about calling you earlier to ask a few questions, then I just figured I'd wait."

"Shoot."

"You said something about Jacob Brown and an argument with the teacher." He turned, leaned his back against the window. "Tell me about that again."

She pivoted on the couch to afford a more comfortable view of Mitch while they talked. "I wouldn't call it an argument exactly. He was just in a foul mood because I was in his class. And it grew fouler when Ms. Daltry praised my writing and called him on his attitude in front of everyone."

"Did he threaten her?"

"No, he just was agitated enough that other students

noticed—one of which commented on his anger, that's all." She searched his face for a clue to his line of questioning but saw nothing. "Why? I thought Ms. Daltry's death was being attributed to the robbery in the computer lab."

She tracked Mitch around the tiny living room with her eyes, aware of his brooding demeanor.

He opened his mouth to speak, stopped, and then started again. "I think it is. But this Jacob connection can't be ignored either."

She felt her mouth gape open, her eyes widen. "What do you mean?"

Mitch shrugged again. "If he's mad at you, he's got to be mad at me."

"Why do you say that?"

"Because I'm the one who actually pulled the trigger. The one who *killed* his dad."

Elise contemplated Mitch's words as her thoughts rewound through their conversation. "Okay, say you're right. Why would he start breaking and entering around town? What does that do?"

Mitch exhaled loudly as he dropped into the single papasan in the corner of the room. "It gets at *me*. It would be like one giant head game…like cat and mouse. A way to test me, taunt me."

There was no getting around it—her reporter persona was intrigued. "I suppose that's possible. Though he still seems like a good kid below all that anger. But let's pretend he's not. He does a few minor break-ins and then goes after the computer lab, killing our teacher in the process. That's kind of taking the cat and mouse game to a sick level, don't you think?"

He met her gaze across the coffee table, concern etched around his eyes and mouth. "I think Hannah Daltry's death was a colossal mistake."

THIRTEEN

1:30 a.m.
Sunday, April 3

THERE WAS NO USE waiting for sleep to descend. It wasn't coming. She'd tried soft music, warm milk, counting sheep, mind-cleansing exercises, and reading. But two hours after climbing into bed she was still wide-eyed.

Recognizing a lost cause, Elise threw back the covers and padded across the thin bedroom carpet on bare feet, the strap of her pink satin camisole slipping down her shoulder. There was always work that could be done—both for the paper and her class—though, in all honesty, none of it held any appeal at the moment.

She'd spent so much energy assuring Mitch she was okay enough for him to leave, that she'd actually fooled herself into believing it. But it wasn't true. The simple fact that Jacob Brown was under a cloud of suspicion for the murder of Hannah Daltry was enough to set her nerves on edge.

Flicking on the living room light, she made a beeline for her laptop computer. With any luck, there would be a few emails to keep her busy until sleep came knocking.

She pressed the power button and waited as the computer slowly booted up, running through the various check screens before finally stopping on the welcome page. A click of the mouse and a password later, she was in her email account—a red seven beside the little yellow mailbox. Just what she needed…

She entered her box and began opening email, taking time to respond to each one, her thoughts slowly taking on a focus other than Jacob Brown.

The first email was from Maureen O'Reilly. Maureen and Elise had become friends during the murder investigation last summer, their relationship deepening in the subsequent months. They got together for lunch every week, shared silly emails with one another in between.

Grateful for the mind-numbing list of questions that were to be answered and then forwarded on to five different friends, she threw herself into coming up with clever replies for each one. Even the standard one word "favorite" answers were embellished with a little wise-cracking. When she was satisfied with her answers she sent it back to Maureen, adding Uncle Ken, his girl-friend Sophie, Jonathan, Aunt Betty, and Mitch to the recipient line.

Next up was an email from Sophie. Ever since she'd met the woman during her vacation to Mackinac Island with Mitch in January, she and the fifty-something-year-old woman had grown very close. It certainly didn't hurt that Sophie and Elise's uncle were engaged to be married. The two couples had joked about a joint wedding here in October, but Ken and Sophie wanted to marry on the island, with Elise's cousin R.J. as Best Man.

She clicked the email open, smiling as she read the latest news on the island…including R.J.'s new job as a groomsman for Stodder's Livery, and Uncle Ken's upcoming showing at the Island Art Gallery. It warmed her heart to hear how happy they all were. Together and at peace.

She jotted a quick reply and pressed send, making a mental note to write a longer letter in a few days— maybe even including tidbits about her teacher's death and the subsequent murder investigation.

The next email in her box was from a sender she didn't recognize: Bestphotog.

Bestphotog? Who on earth—

Dean.

It had to be. Although, it was still hard to accept that the staff photographer was not only *using* a computer but sending email on it now as well. What was next? Computer dating?

She moved the arrow to the blank subject line and double clicked.

Hey Missy. This is your LUCKY day…your email reading life is now complete. I am officially online. Riding the websites and everything.

She giggled. So much for his computer jargon. Maybe she should clue him on the correct terminology.

Then again, maybe not. He could *ride the websites* all he wanted while the rest of the world surfed the net, mocking him.

> **Since I'm new to all this stuff I was wanting to jump in with both feet. While most of my interest lies in the sites we discussed the other day—**

She rolled her eyes and groaned.

> **I'd love to see what one of these forward-of-a-forward things are all about. So pick something fun that you've sent to all your buddies and send it to me too. Okay?**
> **~Dean**

He never ceased to amaze her. Just when she thought she had him all figured out, he did something totally unexpected. Like buy a computer. And get sentimental. Bizarre.

Shrugging, she clicked on her "sent mail" basket and forwarded the goofy question and answer email to him. With any luck he wouldn't pay too much attention to her answers—particularly the ones relating to her favorite food, her favorite way to relax, and her favorite non-work activity. Lord knew what he could do with that kind of information.

The last two emails were Viagra ads and required no action except pressing the delete button without opening.

She stared at her empty mailbox, her needed diversion all but gone. There were websites she could check out, an article on a ribbon cutting ceremony she could start for the paper, her assignment for next week's class to consider, but she opted to shut the computer down instead, her mind still restless.

She pulled the strap of her camisole higher on her shoulder and wandered into the kitchen in search of a dish to put away or a cup to rinse. Unfortunately she was an overachiever most days and it had all been done after Mitch had gone home.

Wandering back into the living room, she shut off the overhead light in favor of a small reading lamp beside the papasan. She pulled Hannah Daltry's dog-eared writing sample from under a nearby pile of books and plopped into the round blue cushion.

It was weird how the same seventeen paragraphs kept calling to her, pulling her back again and again. She'd assumed it was the powerful writing that kept her reading and rereading, but maybe it was just a final connection to a woman brutally murdered for no reason.

Her gaze skimmed down the page.

The black metal cave was cool against my tears...

"She was under a desk. Probably one of the desks inhabited by the people who open new accounts," Elise said aloud, her voice filling the dimly lit room.

The end to Mommy's noises meant we could no longer hear each other...

This made more sense now than it had the first time she read the piece, mainly because Madelyn had explained about the adults being locked in a bank vault during the robbery. She pulled her legs up onto the cushion, hugged her knees with her left arm while holding the paper with her right.

I hugged my legs tighter as I watched their calves pace back and forth, their steps getting faster and crazier with each breath I took.

Desperation. On the part of the robbers *and* little Hannah.

Two of the men wore brown work boots, like Daddy's, the other man wore white sneakers with dark blue squiggles, his laces coming untied like mine always do.

That paragraph was brilliant. Kids make associations, bringing logic to unfamiliar things by likening them to objects and experiences in their own world. But the accuracy made sense knowing that Hannah, the writer, had been the child staring out from under the desk, her mother locked in a vault, unable to soothe the frightened little girl.

She skipped ahead through the next two paragraphs.

But maybe he's afraid. Like me. Or maybe he doesn't know it's okay to play with other people. His mommy should tell him that. And maybe she should tell him it's not nice to scare people too. I bet he'd listen. He seems to be a good listener. Like me.

That part always made her pause, amazed at the empathy a child could show toward someone responsible for her fear. The empathy the adult could still recall thirty-five years later.

She yawned and rubbed at the heaviness in her eyelids, sleep finally starting to take its hold.

I smacked my hand over my mouth to stop from getting excited. Help was coming! Mommy and all the other people would be okay.

The words became blurry on the page as she tried to keep reading, but it was no use. Laying the paper against her chest, she curled into the cushion and closed her eyes.

FOURTEEN

2:30 p.m.

"GOOD HEAVENS, CHILD, I've never seen a waist as tiny as yours. Where do you put your food?"

Elise looked down at Mitch's Aunt Betty and grinned. "Fast metabolism? Crazy hours? A co-worker who routinely steals my snacks?"

"Well, no matter, just make sure you keep doing whatever you're doing for at least another six months." Aunt Betty pulled the satin fabric tightly then motioned to the tailor standing watch by the mirror. "This will do it. It needs to be taken in a good two inches, but if you do it in little amounts it should lay perfectly when you're done."

She knew she shouldn't interrupt the women, but her patience could only hold out so long. "Can I turn around now?"

"Please."

Slowly, she turned on the elevated platform, her gaze purposely avoiding the side mirrors until she could see the entire thing at one time. She looked up as she came to a stop, her mouth gaping open at the woman staring back.

The dress was even more beautiful than it had

appeared on the hanger. The white satin material hugged her slender body in a sexy, feminine way, the crochet-like sleeves ending in a point at her tiny wrists. A hint of tasteful beading complemented the overlay above her chest, and the dress itself pooled at her feet.

Elise moved her hand gently down the fabric, adoring the soft material beneath her skin. It suddenly felt real—more real than it had during any of the other preparations thus far.

Aunt Betty's arm encircled her shoulders and gave her a gentle squeeze. "He will fall in love with you all over again when he sees you in this. You mark my words."

The front door of the bridal shop opened, a breathless voice filling the room over the sound of jingling metal. "Sorry, Margie. They ran out of whole wheat bread for your sandwich so I had to wait while they got some mo—" Their eyes met in the mirror as the girl came around the corner with a white bag in one hand, and a jam-packed key ring in the other. "Oh. Wow. Hey, Elise."

"Hi, Sierra. I didn't know you worked here."

The girl handed the to-go bag to the tailor, dropped her key ring into her coat pocket, and busied herself by straightening a pillow on a chair, a veil on a hook. "I've been here about a year. It's good experience for what I want to do. Certainly better than all those cashier jobs I've worked."

Aunt Betty touched Elise's back and spoke in a hushed voice. "I don't mean to interrupt, dear, but this is a great time to decide how you might want your hair to be with this dress and whether you are going to wear a veil or a wreath or nothing at all."

Nodding, she turned back to the mirror, willed her thoughts to focus on her wedding day rather than the timid girl a few steps away. Besides, if Jacob became a viable suspect in Hannah Daltry's murder, it might be best to keep her distance from his girlfriend during the investigation.

As Mitch's aunt fussed with her dress, she tried out several possibilities for her hair. Her inclination was to wear it down. She wasn't a big fan of changing so much for your wedding day that the groom barely recognized the woman at his side. But the soft curls always looked pretty when they escaped a French twist in face-flattering tendrils.

Elise scooped her hair back and secured it with a clip from Margie. True to form, a curl escaped each side, framing her face with a hint of innocence. "What do you think, Aunt Betty? Should I go with something like this? Or just keep it down like I usually wear it?"

"Oh, that's beautiful just like that. Shows off your high cheekbones and your sparkly eyes." Aunt Betty reached for the pad of paper she'd been jotting notes in for the past hour, adding "French twist" to her running list.

Looking back at her reflection, Elise smiled, imagining the moment she and Mitch exchanged their vows. She simply couldn't wait…

"You look beautiful, Elise."

"What? Oh, thanks." Elise moved her eyes to the

left, found Sierra's reflection looking back. "As soon as I saw this dress I fell in love with it. It's beautiful."

Sierra pushed off the desk she'd been leaning against and walked onto the platform, studying the sleeves and bodice of the dress. "It is beautiful, but you certainly take it up a notch. That's what I want my designs to do. I want them to be exquisite on their own, but be virtually indescribable when the bride-to-be puts them on."

Elise pulled the clip out, letting her hair rain down her back. "Your designs?"

Sierra nodded as she fussed with the dress, helping it to sit even more perfectly across Elise's waist. "I want to be a dress designer. Wedding dresses being my first choice. It's not every day a woman gets to be the center of attention, you know?"

Aunt Betty stepped off the platform and headed over to Margie with the pad of paper in her hand. Elise watched as the elderly woman pointed to a flowered wreath and three different veils before returning with all of them draped across her arm.

"Are you wanting something in your hair or were you thinking of going with nothing?" Aunt Betty slowly cycled through the objects she'd collected, waiting patiently for a response.

Elise looked back at the mirror, at the dress and her hair. "I want something minimal. And I don't want to wear anything in front of my face."

"Try this then." Aunt Betty handed her a wreath and stepped back to see how it looked.

"It's okay. But not exactly right." Elise reached for the smallest of the three veils in Betty's hand and tried it on her head. "No, not this either."

Sierra stepped forward with her index finger bouncing gently on her closed lips. "I think I have an idea. Wait one minute."

In a flash she was gone, disappearing through a door to the left of the mirror and returning a few minutes later. In her hand was a delicate white clip with a thin swath of white netting trailing down from the bottom. "Try this."

Scooping her hair up once again, Elise secured the clip to the back of her head and looked at herself in the mirror. It was exactly what she'd been picturing. "Oh, Sierra, this is perfect. I love it. Thank you."

The girl responded with a shy smile and a shrug. "It looks fabulous on you."

Aunt Betty's face beamed in the mirror as she looked Elise over from head to toe. "Lovely. Absolutely lovely."

She could feel her face growing warm as the three women stared at her, each offering their take on the way she looked. And, being honest, she could hardly believe the way the dress made her look either.

"Okay, now off with it, so Margie can make the necessary alterations." Aunt Betty shooed at her with an empty hand, her words spoken around the pencil in her mouth. "Go."

Giggling softly, she stepped into the suite-like dressing room and closed the door. She couldn't wait for Mitch to see her on their wedding day. To watch his eyes as she walked down the aisle at St. Theresa's.

When the dress was back on its hanger, she slipped into the tan skirt and white sweater she'd worn to church earlier in the day. Aunt Betty had met her after the service, visibly excited to be included in such a special aspect of the wedding preparations. And it was just the way Elise wanted it. The elderly woman had been like a mother to Mitch for the past ten years, stepping in as sole guardian after the death of his parents. She meant the world to him and it wasn't hard to see why.

She stepped into her shoes and stopped in front of the mirror. "You, Elise Jenkins, are one very lucky girl," she whispered.

When she was satisfied with her non-wedding dress appearance, she opened the louvered door and headed toward the front counter. "Okay, Sierra. How much do I owe you today?"

"We take fifty percent today, the remaining fifty percent when you pick it up." Sierra pulled a receipt pad from the top drawer and wrote down the total amount minus the deposit, which Elise paid by check. The cost of the dress meant the next few months would be a little tight financially, but it was well worth it in her eyes. Marrying Mitch Burns was a day to treasure.

"Thank you. Have a great day." Elise looped her purse strap over her shoulder. "I'll see you next Saturday, right?"

"Saturday? Oh, yeah, Saturday. I forgot for a

second." Sierra pulled a notebook from below the countertop and opened the cover. "See? I started working on our next assignment already. Not sure if it's any good, but I'm trying."

Elise picked up the bag with the hair clip. "I'm sure you're doing a great job. I thought the piece you read in class on Saturday was very good. Very real."

Sierra shut the notebook and disappeared below the line of the counter. "Thanks. It was…easy…and hard all at the same time."

Elise thanked Sierra and Margie then followed Aunt Betty onto the sidewalk, falling into step with her as they walked down Sand Castle Road. She linked arms with the woman and planted a light kiss on her cheek. "Thank you, Aunt Betty. For being there with me today. You made me feel beautiful."

The woman stopped walking and turned to face her. "You are beautiful all on your own. Never forget that. And I can't tell you how much I'm looking forward to having you in my family, dear. You and all of your kooky friends."

"Kooky friends?" Elise trotted to keep up with the woman as she set off again in the direction of the car. "I'm not sure I know what you're talking about."

"That Dean fellow you work with. He is truly something else, I tell you. But I like him. He's sweet." Aunt Betty grabbed her hand as they crossed the street toward the lot. "I'm so glad Mitch agreed to come for dinner tonight. It'll be nice having the both of you at my tab—"

"How on earth do you know Dean?" She hadn't

meant to cut the woman off mid-sentence but not a single word had registered in her mind after the photographer's name was mentioned.

Aunt Betty turned the key in the driver's side door and flipped the switch to unlock Elise's side. "By email, of course."

FIFTEEN

6:30 p.m.

IF SHE COULDN'T FIT into her wedding dress in six months, she'd know why. Dinner at Aunt Betty's was like Thanksgiving and Christmas all rolled into one. There was the meat, which, in this case, was roast beef, the various vegetable choices, potatoes, gravy, salads, stuffing, and rolls.

Any hope of working off some calories by shuttling dirty dishes back and forth from the dining room to the kitchen was squelched by a seventy-two year old woman wielding a dish towel like it was a sword and repeating the phrase: *no dishes until after dessert*. And in case she considered disobeying, she was shot the raised-eyebrow-don't-defy-me look that she remembered from her own grandmother.

Sheesh, the elderly could be ornery.

"It's been like this since I was a kid," Mitch whispered in between glances at the kitchen doorway. "You eat and eat until you don't think you can eat again for another ten years. Then she brings out dessert."

"And you still eat it?" she whispered back.

"When she brings out the chocolate cream pie? Are

you kidding me? Of course I eat it. What's another couple pounds in the grand scheme of things, you know?"

"My waistline, that's wha—oh wow, that looks great." Elise sat up in her chair, her eyes widening at the site of the Boston cream pie in Aunt Betty's right hand. She glanced across the table at Mitch and shrugged in surrender.

"Mitch told me you like Boston cream pie so I made one just for you." The woman set the pie plate on the table and disappeared into the kitchen again, returning seconds later with a chocolate cream pie. "And this one is for my Mitchell."

She laughed at Mitch's red face. "*Mitchell*, would you like to try a piece of Boston cream pie, too?"

His lips twitched despite his formal reply. "Why, yes I would, Ms. Jenkins."

Aunt Betty reclaimed her seat, smacking at Elise's knife-holding hand. "I'll cut the pieces. You just relax. You two work so hard all week, the least I can do is make you a nice dinner and keep good food on your plates."

Mitch picked up his butter knife and shook it in Elise's direction. "You better listen, young lady, or that hand smack will be the least of your worries."

The pies were delicious, clearing away any thoughts of full stomachs and too-tight wedding dresses. The conversation was every bit as good, running the gamut from the teenagers in Mitch's law enforcement camp and Elise's news articles, to Aunt Betty's book club.

"I read about that poor woman at the community

college," Aunt Betty said before taking a slow sip of her tea. "That was pretty much the topic of our ladies group meeting on Friday. Seems so sad that two computers could be worth a person's life."

Elise took the last bite of pie into her mouth and met Mitch's eye across the table. It haunted her to know that he felt even the slightest bit responsible for Hannah Daltry's death.

The jovial set to Mitch's mouth changed as he reached toward the pie plate and sheepishly cut a second piece of his favorite. "The loss of life at another person's hand is always sad...especially when quicker movements could have made a difference."

The elderly woman was a sharp cookie who didn't miss so much as an inflection in her nephew's voice. "You are no more responsible for that woman's death than I am. There's only one person who carries that sin. And don't you ever forget that."

Mitch leaned back in his chair ever so slightly and set his fork down beside his plate. "Thanks, Aunt Betty. Most of the time I try to think that way. But other times—when I'm going over the details of the first two robberies—I can't help but think I should have been able to stop it from happening."

"I understand. I think that's natural. Especially for someone like you. But you can't let it overtake your rational side—the side that knows only one person is responsible." Aunt Betty poured some tea into her cup, her head bobbing ever so slightly as she hesitantly continued. "You know, I must admit something, though it may sound foolish."

"What's that?" Mitch asked.

"I wasn't sad to see the first two robberies happen."

Elise looked at Mitch quickly, curious about his reaction to his aunt's odd statement. The look of shock on his face mirrored what she felt inside.

The woman held up her hands before either could speak. "Wait. Let me explain. If you think about it, those fortune teller murders from last year *still* seem to creep their way into the news. It never ends. It's always there in one way or the other. At least the robberies gave the television reporters something else to chew on for a little while."

"Yeah, but—"

"Ah, don't mind me, Mitchell. I'm just an old lady babbling away." Aunt Betty sat forward, added a touch of sugar to her tea cup, then trained her focus on Elise. "Is it hard to be covering another murder so soon?"

She wiped her mouth with the cloth napkin from her lap and shrugged gently. "I don't enjoy these kinds of stories very much to begin with, but this one is a little harder because I knew the victim."

Aunt Betty gasped, her eyes jumping to Mitch with worry.

"Oh no, don't worry." Elise covered the elderly woman's hand with her own and squeezed ever so gently. "I didn't know her well, or even for any length of time. But what I saw, I liked."

"How did you know her, dear?"

Elise scooted back her chair just a little and crossed her legs. "Ms. Daltry was my teacher for a creative writing class I just started taking. In fact, she was found just two days after my class met for the very first time."

The woman shook her head softly and *tsked* under her breath. "So sad. Did she seem very nice?"

"Oh yes, she did. She was a fireball, so enthusiastic about writing and about getting everyone else fired up as well." Elise took a sip from her water goblet and lingered her hand on the stem even after setting it down. "She started off the class by pointing at various students and describing things about them that would set mood, tone in a story. It was really interesting."

"Good teachers always stand out, don't they, Mitchell?" Aunt Betty warmed her hands against her teacup and peered across the table. "Remember that teacher you had your senior year of high school? The one who helped you after Mom and Dad died? What was his name again?"

"Mr. Filo. Jerry Filo. He was my history teacher. He was phenomenal."

Elise studied him as he talked, noting the way his eyes took on a faraway look as if he was transferring himself back in time.

"I wasn't a big fan of history to begin with, not a huge fan of school at that particular time in my life. Things were just too heavy, you know?"

Elise nodded and waited for him to continue.

"Anyway, Mr. Filo taught this more modern day kind of history. No Early European or pilgrim period stuff. He taught about events we weren't necessarily alive for, but seemed more recent because we'd heard our parents or grandparents talk about them." Mitch shoveled the last piece of his second pie into his mouth and swallowed quickly. "And we didn't have books. He just lectured and we listened. It was like listening to a story instead of being lectured at. He asked what *we* wanted to learn. We thought he was nuts. But we threw something out anyway.

"For the next two days, Mr. Filo sat at his desk researching the Manson murders. The background, the whys, the theories, the victims, you name it. Then he taught it to us. He made it come alive, made us feel as if we were there."

Elise smiled as she watched her fiancé's face light up at the memory.

"When that was done, we requested the Kennedy assassination, the Lindberg kidnapping, and Vietnam. He'd research for a few days, then teach us. Never, in all my years of school, did I enjoy a class that much. And it was because of Mr. Filo."

The room was quiet for a moment, each silent in their own thoughts, their own memories. Finally, Aunt Betty spoke.

"What else did you like about Ms. Daltry, Elise?"

Fueled by Mitch's enthusiasm for his history teacher, Elise could feel herself getting excited. "She was an amazing writer. She could make her work come alive, pull you into what was happening in such a way that you forgot you were *reading*."

Now it was Mitch who leaned back in his chair, smiling as she talked. It made her blush.

"And you'd like to write like that?"

Elise pulled her gaze from Mitch's and addressed his aunt. "I like journalism very much, but I'd love to write a novel someday. A mystery probably. I like creating a world that is so detailed and so engaging that the reader can escape inside it until the very end."

"I love those kinds of stories too," Aunt Betty said, her mouth widening in a smile. "I read a book the other day that took place in a castle. The author described it so well I could almost smell the musty rooms."

"Exactly." Elise shifted in her seat and took another sip of water. "You should see the piece Ms. Daltry shared with us as an example for our first assignment. It was mind-blowing. Never once did it say anything about a bank robbery or a vault or anything that was a dead giveaway to the location. But you knew what was happening, you knew that the little girl was terrified because she put us there…under the desk…*with her*."

"Whoa. Is that the thing you were telling me about on the phone that one night? The writing sample?" Mitch pushed his empty plate forward a few inches and rested his elbows on the table.

"Yes."

"You said it was a real experience from her childhood, didn't you?"

She nodded. "It was. Madelyn—a woman in my class—says she thinks Ms. Daltry must have been a witness to a bank robbery in Paleville thirty-five years ago even though it was never reported in the news."

"That's the kind of thing most departments will keep to themselves. Safety for the child and a piece of information that could help them." Mitch rested his chin in his palm and smiled at Elise. "Did she see the guys? Was she able to I.D. them?"

"According to Madelyn, two of the three were shot and killed on the way out of the bank that day. The other got away. But no, she couldn't I.D. them anyway because they were wearing masks and gloves."

Mitch sat back and ran a finger along the lace design of the tablecloth. "I guess she was able to work through that experience by writing about it."

"Yeah, I think so too. It was amazing. But kinda sad also."

"Why's that?"

Elise laced her fingers together and set them in her lap. "Think about it. She witnessed a robbery when she was just seven years old. She got out alive by being quiet." She cleared her throat quickly and continued. "Thirty-five years later she wasn't quite so lucky."

Mitch tossed his napkin onto the table and stood, reaching for Elise's plate. "Fate seems kind of cruel sometimes, doesn't it?"

She reached for the pie plates and was shooed from them by Aunt Betty. "No. You are my guest this evening. Sit."

It was hard to argue with that eyebrow, but she did anyway. "Please, I feel uncomfortable sitting here while you clean up. Let me at least help carry some plates into the kitchen." She flashed a grin at the woman. "It'll be exercise. To make sure the dress will still fit."

Aunt Betty shoved a plate into her hand and pointed her finger at the kitchen. "What are you waiting for then? Go!"

SIXTEEN

9:00 a.m.
Monday, April 4

ELISE LOOKED DOWN at her notebook and the story suggestions she'd jotted down before bed. They were all good, solid ideas. But there was one that excited her more than all the rest. One that would enable her to explore a piece of local history that had been kept secret for so long.

"What's shaking, missy?" Dean dropped into the seat across from her and propped his feet on the conference table. "Mitchy home safe and sound?"

"Nothing. And yes."

"Ooooohhhh. Aren't we in a snippy mood? Things amiss in the love nest?" The photographer leaned back in his chair, resting his head in his hands and studying her through narrowed eyes.

She reached down to the bag held in place by her knees and pulled out the blue package, careful to keep it hidden from his line of vision. "Things are wonderful, thankyouverymuch. I was simply answering your questions. Nothing is shaking. And yes, *Mitch* is home safe and sound. How is that snippy?"

Dean rolled his eyes then stopped, his nose lifting in the air, his ears seeming to prick forward. "Hold it. Hold it. There's food in this room."

She giggled.

"E-lise? What do you have?" He dropped his feet to the ground and reached across the table, patted her left hand with his own. "What's your other hand doing?"

"What other hand?"

"The right one. The one that's under the table making occasional crinkling noises."

"This one?" She set the package on her thighs and raised her hand above the table. "It's not doing anything, see?"

Shrugging, he pulled his arm back and started to lean back in his chair again but dove under the table instead. She tried to move fast enough, but it was no use. Dean Waters was one fast dude when food was at the finish line.

"Ah ha! Is that a package of Chips Ahoy! cookies I see?"

"What? These?" She pulled the package from her lap and set them on the table, laughing at the loud thump that followed. The site of Dean climbing back into his chair and rubbing his head added a snort to her reaction. "Do you *like* chocolate chip cookies, Dean? I didn't know that."

His hand paused mid-rub as he straightened in his chair and met her gaze. "Wow. Who taught you how to play hardball, missy?"

"You."

"Okay. Yeah. That makes sense. Because you're getting better at it all the time." His words grew somewhat muffled as he hoisted his camera bag onto the table and unzipped the front pouch, removing a Caramello bar with a slow, theatrical hand. "Whoa. Would you look at this? Seems such a shame to let chocolate and caramel go to waste, doesn't it?"

She licked her lips and shifted in her seat.

"You okay, missy? You're starting to foam around the mouth."

Damn. When was she going to remember there was no tangling with the beast?

Focus, Elise. Focus.

"Would you like some cookies, Dean?" It took every ounce of willpower she had to force her gaze from the candy bar to the photographer's face.

"I don't want *some*. I want the whole package."

Her gaze drifted back to the Caramello bar. "Wait a minute. That's *my* candy bar, isn't it? I have one of those stashed in my desk for an emergency."

"*Had*. You *had* one of those stashed in your desk for an emergency." Dean ran his fingers across the wrapped bar, his lashes batting ever so sweetly in her direction. "But I believe it is in my possession now, is it not?"

"You fink!"

"Now that's not any way for a nice young lady like yourself to talk, is it? Would Uncle Ken approve?"

Her mouth dropped open. First, Aunt Betty. Now, Uncle Ken? What in the world was he blabbering about?

"Your mouth hanging open like that, love, is not one of your better looks. Trust me." Dean bent his fingers inward and began filing his nails with the wrapped candy bar, his face void of expression.

"How do you know Uncle Ken?"

"Great guy. Helluva photographer too."

Her nostril flared.

"I take it that package of cookies was meant to be a bribe of some sort? So what were the stakes? I'm curious."

"Um, I uh—"

"Good morning, you two. Where's Tom and Karen?" Sam walked into the conference room, set his binder on the table, and glanced at his wrist watch. "Oh crap. My watch is dead."

Dean extended his right arm in the boss's direction and tapped at it with the candy bar. "It's nine-fifteen."

"Wow, Dean, that's a real beaut. What'd that set you back? Twenty, maybe thirty bucks?" Sam walked back to the doorway and popped his head out, looking down the tiny hallway in both directions before returning to his spot.

Pulling his arm inward, Dean busied himself with the candy bar. "Yeah, probably," he mumbled as he began flying the candy through the air in front of him, bringing it closer and closer to his mouth.

Looking from Elise and her cookies, to Dean and the candy bar, the balding man simply shook his head and raised his palms upward. "I'm not even gonna ask."

"Hey, guys." Tom Miller breezed into the room,

claiming a chair to the left of Elise. "Great sweater, Elise. Very pretty color on you."

Just when she thought the day couldn't get more bizarre…

"Thanks, Tom." She ran her free hand across her cheeks, felt them warming beneath her skin. Catching Dean's brief look of surprise didn't help. Especially when he traced the shape of a heart on the table with the edge of the candy bar.

Gggrrrreeeaaattttt.

The grand entrance of Karen Smith (aka the prima donna of the print world as Sam fondly referred to the society reporter) was a welcome diversion in a room that had suddenly become stifling. Elise turned in her seat and greeted the platinum blonde with an uncharacteristic rush of enthusiasm. To which she received a raised eyebrow in return.

Dean's lips simply twitched as he slowly unwrapped the Caramello bar. "Mmmmm…I'm hungry this morning."

"Okay, guys. Times a wastin'. Let's get this show on the road." Their fearless leader took his place at the head of the table and opened his binder. "Great paper yesterday, everyone."

Sam eyed Elise first. "Your story on Hannah Daltry's murder was well done. You did a great job getting the facts as we know them into the story, yet refraining from needless guessing."

Dean was next.

"That photograph of the body being carried out was very tasteful. We knew it was there, could sense the gravity of the situation without it being crammed down the reader's throat. Excellent."

Dean patted himself on the back and took a slow, deliberate bite of the chocolate bar, dramatic moans and groans accompanying each chew. "Mmmmmm. Elise. You would lllooovvve this candy bar. Love. It."

She'd always prided herself on the fact that she was a non-violent person. A strong believer in communication as the best solution to a difference of opinion or a disagreement. But not today. In fact, if she didn't think it would ruffle a few feathers, she'd climb across the table and wrap her fingers around the photographer's scrawny little neck.

Correction.

The photographer's scrawny and *chocolate-flecked* neck. Uggh.

Sam shook his head and continued. "Tom, I heard some scuttlebutt at my men's group meeting last night. Seems St. T.'s is looking at bringing in a coach from northern Jersey instead of going with one of McMahan's assistants. You heard that?"

The sports reporter pulled out his notebook and started jotting notes, his face tensing as he wrote. "No. I haven't. But I will find out now."

"Karen. Fun piece on the Spring Fling at town hall. I always knew those folks could party, but had no idea just how much." Sam looked down at his notes and then back up at his staff. "Now, what do you all have for me? How are we going to make this next paper even better?"

"I could get a picture of 'Lisey's perfect pout over there. Put it next to Councilman Robert's mug and we'd have a matched set." Dean crammed the last of the candy bar into his mouth and burped.

She debated on whether to make a face or return a clever retort. But Tom beat her to the punch.

"Lay off, Dean."

Uh oh. Now he was defending her. Not a good sign.

Dean looked from Elise to Tom and back again, his lashes batting all the more furiously at Elise as he pursed his lips.

Ggggrrrreeeeeaaatttttt.

Embarrassed beyond belief, she forced herself to ignore the empty wrapper clutched in the photographer's hand, willed herself to find another reason for Tom's protective reply than the one that was becoming most clear. "Um, I've got some ideas for this week. One of which I'd really like to get on right away."

She looked up at Sam, felt the pleading in her gaze. If she could distract Dean long enough, she could get her assignment and spend most of the day away from the office. Far away. An important ingredient if she was going to be spared a manslaughter charge.

"What do you have, hon?" Sam folded his hands and waited.

"I'd like to change up the basic murder story a little by delving into the victim's past. In particular, an aspect that many people may remember but have no clue she was tied to."

Dean quit fiddling with the wrapper and leaned forward, his curiosity obviously aroused.

"The robbery?" Sam asked.

She nodded. "Yeah. I want to bring in the way the police hold back certain aspects of any crime and why. I want to bring in how children work through traumatic instances...talk to a child psychologist."

"I like it. A lot. It's different. It's something we have an inside track on thanks to your participation in Hannah's class. And the different aspects you just mentioned could turn this into an extended news feature. Several stories all pulling together into the main one."

"What's the deal? What robbery? What does that have to do with the victim?" Dean asked.

"Thirty-five years ago there was a bank robbery in Paleville. Hannah Daltry, then seven-years-old, hid under a desk during the entire thing—unnoticed by the suspects as they went about robbing the bank."

"Why would a little girl be in a bank alone?" Karen *tsked* aloud, her face contorted in disgust. "Some parents just never cease to amaze me."

"It wasn't like that, Karen." Elise turned her head and addressed the rigid woman at the other end of the table. "Her mother was there. And so were other people. They were locked in a vault the entire time."

Dean whistled under his breath. "Interesting. Can I get in on this? Take some pictures of the bank?"

Oh how she'd love to tell him to shove it. But she couldn't. First, the accompanying photographs would be sensational, especially if they could illustrate the hiding place of the little girl. But, more than the benefit to the paper, she simply couldn't stay mad at Dean. He was certainly quirky, annoying, and totally obnoxious. No one would dispute that. He just happened to be fun to hang around with as well.

Besides, she still had the cookies to hang over his head while she tried to figure out his motives for contacting her loved ones…

"Most definitely. Pictures would be great. Just let me do the legwork first so we know what direction to go with. Okay?"

Surprisingly, he agreed. Easily.

"Why don't you talk to Hannah's mother? She could probably give you a whole different perspective on what the child went through after that event. And how—if any—it affected her into adulthood."

It was exhilarating when Sam jumped into a story idea with both feet. His instincts took over and his suggestions were always outstanding. Today was certainly no exception.

"I love it!" Elise began to write the contact name down, then stopped. "But do you think it would be too upsetting? It's only been a week."

Sam leaned over his chair and pulled a sheet of paper from his briefcase. "Here is Mrs. Daltry's address at the assisted living facility in Paleville. I talked to her over the weekend to explain about the paychecks she'd be receiving from my work at the college. She's heartbroken, of course. But I think she was buoyed by the opportunity to talk about her daughter. If you handle this in the gentle and classy manner you always handle these kinds of stories, you'll be fine."

"Thanks, Sam."

SEVENTEEN

2:15 p.m.

THE PALEVILLE POLICE DEPARTMENT was bigger than Ocean Point's. Bigger building, more officers, larger fleet of cars, and a definite increase in background noise. She may even have felt a tad bit overwhelmed if it hadn't been for Mitch's phone call to his counterpart, paving the way for her visit.

Elise tried to focus on the list of questions she'd compiled for Detective Brunetti before leaving the office. But it was hard to concentrate with a handcuffed man in an orange jumpsuit sitting across from her in the waiting area, eyeing her from head to toe. Oddly, she was aware that her feelings were a mixture of unease and excitement. What did he do? And why?

The crime beat was one she both enjoyed and loathed. When it presented a puzzle—like a murder whodunit—it was hard not to feel her adrenaline pumping, her curiosity increasing. When it meant recording basic crime facts with no opportunity to delve further, it was tedious at best.

"Ms. Jenkins?"

She jumped to her feet, her notebook sliding to the floor. As she bent to pick it up, she traded glances with the suspect, a shiver running down her spine. He opened his mouth and snapped it shut, his eyes toying with her as she hurried to the receptionist's desk.

Smoothing her skirt and tugging at her sweater, Elise took a slow, deliberate breath and focused on the thirty-something woman behind the counter with coal-black hair and dark brown eyes. "I'm Ms. Jenkins."

"Detective Brunetti will see you now." The woman pushed a button on the wall, prompting a buzzing sound as the door to the left of her desk unlatched. "Just go through that door. His office is the fifth one on the right."

The hallway was painted a muted grey and had a series of doors leading off of it on both sides, a stark contrast to the handful of private offices in the Ocean Point department. She proceeded down the narrow linoleum floor, counting doorways in her mind. One, two, three, four…

Five. A thin brown wall placard bore the name: Douglas Brunetti, Detective. She knocked on the open door, studying the man behind the desk as she did.

Douglas Brunetti was about forty-five years old. Even seated at his desk, Elise could tell he—like Mitch—was trim and in shape, a complete antithesis of the cliché donut-eating image that often went with his profession. Maybe detectives were different, she mused.

The man looked up, smiled as he saw her standing in the doorway. "You must be Elise," he said, rising from his chair and crossing the distance between them in mere seconds. "Detective Burns told me to be on the lookout for you. He just neglected to tell me how easy you'd be to spot."

"Can I bring you home with me?" she laughed, instantly feeling at home with the man Mitch described as a hard-working, honest guy. "Thanks for agreeing to talk to me today. I won't take too much of your time."

Waving his hand in the air, Detective Brunetti motioned to the empty leather chair beside his desk. "Take a seat. Can I get you anything? Coffee? Soda? Water?"

"No, thank you. I stopped at the diner a few blocks away before I got here. Gave me a chance to get my questions in order." Elise set her purse on the floor and sat down. "How long have you been a detective here?"

He resumed his spot behind the desk, pushing his paperwork off to the side. "About five years. But I've been with the department for five before that."

She nodded as she jotted his answer down. "I realize you were just a child yourself, but are you familiar with the bank robbery that happened here thirty-five years ago?"

"Absolutely." Detective Brunetti picked his right foot off the ground and rested it across his left knee. "It was at that moment that I decided to be a police officer when I grew up. I was fascinated with the whole thing. The excitement. The how. The who. The why."

She got that. It's how her desire to write was born. It hit her early in life, taking hold and never letting go.

"There was more to that bank robbery than people realize, wasn't there?"

He quirked his eyebrows and cocked his head. "How so?"

"There was someone else in that bank besides the people in the vault and the three robbers."

"Tell me what you know." He was intrigued; she could see it in his face.

"A seven-year-old girl by the name of Hannah Daltry was hiding under a desk during the robbery."

For a moment Detective Brunetti said nothing. He simply shifted a puff of air around in his closed mouth for a few moments while he contemplated the conversation. Finally, he spoke.

"Yes, she was. May I ask how you know that?"

Elise reached into her purse and extracted the writing sample, handing it to the detective. "Hannah Daltry was my writing instructor at Ocean Point Community College. She wrote about the robbery in an example for the class. With the help of an older student, we were able to put two and two together."

She watched as the detective's eyes skimmed down the page, his face curious as he stopped at the bottom and went back to the top, working his way through the story one more time. When he spoke, his voice was quiet yet strong.

"We were all sad to hear of her murder. Hannah was a neat kid, I mean, woman."

Her ears perked. "Did you know Hannah when you were kids?"

The detective nodded. "Yes. She lived across the street from me. She was about seven when all that happened, I think. I was ten."

The connection was one she hadn't even imagined uncovering. Feeling her heart rate begin to accelerate, she leaned forward, oblivious to the list of questions in her lap. "Did you know she'd been in there?"

Again, he nodded. "I did. But the only reason I knew is because my mom and Mrs. Daltry were best friends. And I overheard Hannah's mom telling mine."

"That was a lot for a kid to absorb, I bet."

"It was. But I could also tell how important it was that word never got out. So I never uttered a sound about it to anyone. I hated the idea that a little kid I'd known her whole life had been scared by three thugs, as my mom called them. I think that was the real moment I knew I wanted to be a cop."

She tossed his words around in her mind for a few seconds, letting it all sink in and take hold. "You ever tell anyone you knew?"

"Nope. Not my mom. Not my dad. Not even Hannah. I just kept a close watch on her at school and in the neighborhood. She seemed real removed after it happened. Sad. I think she took it far harder than this writing sample shows." He looked at the page one last time and then handed it back to Elise. "But she rebounded nicely. Set her path on teaching when she left high school and made a nice career for herself."

"Why do you think it was kept a secret?"

"Her safety, I guess. I've looked at the records from back then. Studied the case. Would love nothing more than to find the loser who got away. But after so many years and so little physical evidence, the likelihood is slim to none."

Her pen moved across her notepad, working desperately to get everything down. "Little evidence?"

"As she said in her writing, they wore masks and gloves. No fingerprints. He got off scot-free."

"And the money?"

"It was all recovered at the scene. The guy dropped his bag and ran when his buddies got shot. And in the chaos of those initial moments with gunfire and bodies dropping, he slipped away."

Glancing down at her list of questions, she got back on track. "I understand the child safety thing in this instance, I guess. But when a child isn't involved, what makes you hold back certain bits of information after a crime? And how do you know what to hold back?"

"Good question." He pulled open a drawer to his left and pulled out a thick binder. "See this? It's supposed to be like a detective bible of sorts. You know…how to do things and when. But a lot of the times, I don't use it." He dropped it back in his drawer and turned back to Elise. "It's more instinctual. I imagine Mitch would tell you the same thing."

"What you hold back from the public can often be what breaks a case, can't it?" she asked.

He nodded. "Yes, it can. If we hold back a particular pattern we see between murders, and we question someone who mentions that pattern or some bit of information we've kept to ourselves...then bingo, we've got our man. Or, at the very least, someone who knows something about the crime and can potentially lead us where we need to go."

She veered from her prepared questions once again. "Could there have been any other reason Hannah's presence in that bank was kept quiet?"

Detective Brunetti seemed to ponder her question as he turned a pen over and over on his desk. "I don't think so. The reports I read never said she knew anything. You know. You saw what she wrote. She was scared. They wore masks. She tried to stay out of their line of vision which means her visual on them was limited. I don't think she knew enough to ever I.D. anyone if that's what you're thinking. But they'd still keep her presence quiet simply because a criminal could get spooked."

"I guess that makes sense. But—" she stopped, fiddled with her pen for a moment, then regained eye contact. "If that robbery took place today, with you as detective, would you have done anything differently?"

Detective Brunetti tented his fingers to his lips and sat silently for a few moments, seeming to mull over her question with an intensity she wouldn't have expected. But it made sense. This crime had touched his life directly.

"I think the main thing would have been in relation to Hannah. I would have brought a child psychologist in to work with her. Not necessarily to grill her, but to help her work through her experiences. At the very least, it would have helped her. At best, it may have uncovered something no one realized was there."

"They didn't do that?"

"We are more aware of how crimes like that impact victims these days. That awareness wasn't always there thirty-five years ago."

"Do you see any reason why I can't write about her presence in that bank now? In light of her death?"

Detective Brunetti studied her for a long moment, an internal assessment that made her feel neither uncomfortable nor irritated. The Hannah connection was a secret the Paleville Police Department had kept from the press for thirty-five years. And, more importantly, it was a secret he'd kept since he, himself, was a child.

"Mitch had nothing but good things to say about you as a reporter. He said you're more than fair with his department and that you write with compassion. Between that and what my own vibes tell me, I'm good with it. Hannah was forced to hold that experience in for much too long. I do have one request, though."

She was honored both by what Mitch had said as well as Detective Brunetti's willingness to give her the benefit of the doubt. "Anything."

"Run it by Mrs. Daltry first. Make sure it's okay with her."

Elise set her notepad on the desk and stood, extending her hand to the detective. "I have an appointment to sit down and talk with Mrs. Daltry tomorrow morning.

I'd never dream of telling this part of Hannah's story without her permission."

Her hand disappeared inside his warm, firm grasp. "Thank you, Elise."

EIGHTEEN

10:30 a.m.
Tuesday, April 5

FOR THE SECOND DAY in a row, Elise made the thirty minute trek out to Paleville, New Jersey. But this time she drove past the diner and the police department, turning down a small side street bordered by massive dogwood trees waiting for spring to bring their blooms.

She was both excited and apprehensive about her meeting with Genevieve Daltry. If there was anyone who knew what young Hannah had gone through following her ordeal in the bank, it would be her mother. The insights the woman could provide would be invaluable in writing her article. But sitting down with the loved one of a victim was always hard. Their grief was new, raw. And Elise's sensitive nature usually left her crying as well.

Slowing at the first stop sign, she looked ahead and to the right, the soft yellow corner of the Paleville Gardens Assisted Living Apartments peeking out from behind a row of still-bare maple trees just as the receptionist had described. It was a beautiful setting with walking trails and small ponds, park benches and picnic pavilions scattered across the well manicured grounds of the facility. The kind of place where the elderly deserved to live after a lifetime of hard work.

She maneuvered her car into a parking spot and grabbed her backpack purse with her notebook and pen inside. The list of questions she'd compiled for Hannah's mother was very different from the one she'd made yesterday for Detective Brunetti.

Several residents were sitting on a bench beside the front door, enjoying the unseasonably warm day as Elise approached.

"Good morning, it sure is a beautiful day, isn't it?" She stopped and admired the small basket one woman was weaving. "Wow, you do great work."

The cotton-topped woman of about eighty grinned from the praise. "Thank you. I've been making baskets since I was knee-high. My grandmother Rosetti taught me."

"Well you were a good student." Elise hoisted her backpack purse a bit higher on her arm. "Can you tell me where to find Genevieve Daltry? Is there a place I need to check in before I can visit?"

A frail man with a grey cap and a loose fitting sweater nodded. "Genevieve is in apartment 2B. Are you here to spend a little time with her?"

Elise nodded. "I am."

She strained to hear the man as he continued, his words soft yet well spoken. "Good. Genevieve has been through so much this week. She misses her Hannah terribly. If you bring that ray of sunshine you have on your face, that should help a little." The man lifted his wrinkled hand from his lap and grasped Elise's. "A warm smile can make a world of difference sometimes."

Good advice no matter what the circumstance. Thanking them for their time, Elise walked over to the large glass doors, stepped inside as they swished open.

A short, stout woman looked up from behind a desk just inside the entranceway. "May I help you?"

"Yes, please. I'm here to see Genevieve Daltry in apartment 2B."

The woman tilted her head downward and peered at Elise over the top rim of her glasses. "Is Mrs. Daltry expecting you?"

"She is. My name is Elise Jenkins."

"Just one moment." Dorothy—according to the tag on her shirt—flipped through a thin stack of notes, stopping when she came to one with a pink border. "Why yes, here we go. This says that you are welcome to go straight down to her apartment."

Elise smiled at Dorothy. "Thank you."

The woman lowered her voice, looking to both sides before speaking. "Mrs. Daltry could use a little company. It's been hard for her this week. We've all spoken with her, expressed our sympathies upon the death of her daughter, but it's hard to know what to say sometimes. And we're all grieving in our own ways. Hannah was a delight. Everyone here loved her."

There was nothing to do but nod. If she said anything

more, she might get teary-eyed herself. It had been that way her whole life. She'd cry over a dead cat in the road. Wipe her eyes at the end of the Miss America pageant. It didn't matter what it was, but she felt people's hurt and joy deep inside. Having known the victim herself just brought that emotion up a notch.

"She was, indeed, special." Elise started to step away from the counter, then stopped. "How do I find her apartment?"

"Oh, I'm sorry. I just get to talking sometimes." Dorothy came from behind the counter and pointed down a hallway to her left. "Go to the end and turn right. Mrs. Daltry's apartment will be the second from the end off that second hallway."

She thanked the woman then made her way in the direction of apartment 2B. Each door along the route was decorated a bit differently. Some had a wreath, some a welcome sign, others a door hanger…all giving a quick glimpse of the personality that lived inside.

When she reached Genevieve Daltry's closed door, she inhaled slowly and waited a few moments before knocking. She wanted to be a positive force in the elderly woman's day, not one that brought more pain.

Realizing she was as ready as she'd ever be, she raised her fist and knocked softly. Once, twice.

The door slowly opened and a woman roughly two inches shorter than Elise appeared. Her soft grey hair was neatly styled in a bob, her warm hazel eyes glistened with moisture. "Yes?"

"Mrs. Daltry, I'm Elise Jenkins, we spoke yesterday?" She shifted from foot to foot hoping the woman would remember their telephone conversation.

"Jenkins. Jenkins." A look of understanding filtered across her face, followed by a slight smile. "Of course, yes. Please come in."

Genevieve stepped to the side and motioned Elise into her tiny but tastefully-decorated apartment. "I'm sorry for the mess."

Elise grasped the woman's hand and held it gently. "Please, everything is fine. I'm here to see *you*."

"I miss my Hannah so much," Genevieve's voice broke as the woman worked to regain her composure. "She was one-of-a-kind."

Following Hannah's mother over to the sitting room, Elise perched on the edge of a floral wing chair. "As I explained to you on the phone yesterday, I only met your daughter once—on the first day of my creative writing class. But she was wonderful. So enthusiastic. So encouraging. I am sad that I won't get to know her better."

The woman disappeared into a room off the living room and returned with two books. One appeared to be an album, the other something homemade and tied together with red ribbons. She sat on the corner of the sofa closest to Elise. "Let me help you do just that."

Page by page they looked through the photo album, a gift from Hannah the previous Mother's Day. Each page was laid out in a theme that corresponded with the pictures, three to four for each year of their life together.

There was Hannah as an infant in the hospital, Hannah learning to walk on the beach for the very first time. Birthday parties and holidays followed, the first day of kindergarten on a page of its own.

"Hannah was such a good student from the very beginning. Always eager to learn. Eager to grow." Genevieve ran a thin, wrinkly finger across a picture of a smiling Hannah of about six or seven. "She loved life. Was always so happy, so trusting, so centered. And then it changed."

"Changed?" Elise bent over the page they'd stopped on, smiling at the little girl making angels in the snow.

"Yes. Being separated from me that day terrified her. She was never quite the same after that."

Elise snapped her head up, realizing that Genevieve was referring to the robbery.

"Sure, she was still happy and giving. But something had changed. There was a sadness that would creep up unexpectedly. Sometimes she'd talk to me, share her fears. But sometimes she'd disappear into her room and escape into the pages of a book." The woman slipped her arms into a sweater and pulled it close to her body.

She waited to see if Hannah's mother would continue, unsure of whether she should question her now or give her more time to feel comfortable.

"As time went by, Hannah stopped talking about it completely. She focused her attention on her writing and her schooling. I thought she'd put it behind her, moved on. But if she wrote about it for your class as you told me on the phone, then I was sadly mistaken." Genevieve pulled her gaze off the album and met Elise's, the lines around her eyes deepening with grief. "Did you bring the essay with you?"

Patting her purse, Elise nodded. "I did. Would you like to see it?"

The woman's lips trembled as they stretched outward in a tentative smile. "Oh yes, please. Very much."

Elise pulled her purse onto her lap and extracted the folded sheet of paper. "I've read this so many times over the past week I feel as if I have it memorized. Your daughter was an amazingly gifted writer."

Genevieve took the paper from Elise's hand and slowly unfolded it, her hands shaking with each movement. It was heartbreaking to watch, yet Elise couldn't help but sense there was a feeling of anticipation and excitement emanating from the woman.

She looked down at her hands intertwined in her lap, anxious to give the woman a few moments alone with her daughter's words. Words she was reading for the very first time.

After several long minutes, the woman cleared her throat and held the page toward Elise. "This is the first time I feel as if I've been inside her head since it happened. She'd told me in quiet moments during the days and months that followed that she'd been scared. But reading this actually put me in her heart. Thank you."

Elise put her hand against Genevieve's. "No. Please.

You keep it. I can get a copy from one of my fellow classmates. I'd like you to have this."

Hannah's mother covered her mouth with her hand as a few tears quietly slipped down her cheeks. After a long, silent pause, she spoke, her words slightly garbled and shaky. "Thank you. I will treasure it. Always."

Desperate to help the woman, Elise focused on the homemade book tied together by red ribbons. "What's that? It looks special."

Genevieve closed her eyes briefly, wiped at the tears with the back of her small, bony hand. When she opened them again, she nodded. "It is."

Shifting the photo album to the empty sofa cushion beside her, Genevieve replaced it with the homemade book of colorful pages. "When Hannah was about ten or eleven, she started writing. Story books, essays, poems, short stories, you name it, she wrote it.

"Looking back now, I think it was about that same point that she stopped talking about her experience. Perhaps her writing provided a needed escape…a way to forget. I certainly hope so."

Elise reached for the woman's hand again. "I bet it did. My writing does that for me as well. It's helped me through some tough patches in my life. Sometimes consciously, sometimes unconsciously. But always welcome."

The woman nodded. Her eyes were a little less sad as she smiled at Elise and placed her free hand on top of both of theirs. "I'm glad you came today. It's helped more than you can know."

She could feel her eyes stinging, a lump in her throat forming. "I'm so glad."

They sat that way for a few moments, each content to be in each other's presence. Elise, because she was helping. Genevieve, she suspected, because it was a chance to talk about her beloved daughter.

Finally, the woman inhaled deeply and straightened her shoulders. "Now, what can I do for you?"

Elise fiddled with the hem of her skirt, then let it drop back to her legs as she reached for her notepad and pen. "Why did the police keep Hannah's presence in the bank quiet? Surely the third suspect would have known she couldn't identify him, right?"

"True. His face was covered. The likelihood of her identifying him was next to nothing." Genevieve leaned back slowly, rested her back against the sofa, her words soft and faraway as she seemed to slip back thirty-five years. "But the police felt the man could simply get spooked, react irrationally. Though, my feeling was always that he'd put as much distance between himself and Paleville as possible."

A question popped in her head as the woman spoke, one that had no real significance yet suddenly seemed so important. Blatant curiosity, no doubt. "Mrs. Daltry? Hannah differentiated between the three men in her writing. Do you know which man got away?"

Elise watched as the woman tipped her head back and closed her eyes, her slim mouth nibbled inward on one side. When she reopened them, she looked down at her daughter's words. "I'm sad to say she never talked about that day in this much detail with me. I knew there were three. I always knew she thought one of them had been scared. But I didn't know she'd tagged them by impressions.

"But now that I see her words, I'm fairly certain it was the one she calls..." Genevieve ran her finger down the page, stopping at the fifth paragraph, "Blue Squiggle Man."

"Why?" Elise asked quickly.

"Because the other two—the ones who were shot and killed—were still lying on the sidewalk when the rest of us were removed from the building. The two men were covered by sheets, but their feet must have been showing because Hannah whispered something about the Work Boot Guys. I just never understood what she meant until just now."

She leaned forward, anxious to hear as much detail as possible. "Do you remember what she said?"

Genevieve nodded. "I do. It came rushing back when you asked your question. I had my arm around her shoulders and a police officer was on her other side...trying to shield her from seeing too much. I remember her feet slowing down...seeing her look over her shoulder as we passed the sheets. She said, 'Work Boot Guys weren't as fast this time.'"

It may have been highly inappropriate, but she laughed softly at Hannah's words. Not out of disrespect, but simply because they fit perfectly with the little girl in the story. "I'm sorry, Mrs. Daltry, I'm not laughing at the situation. It just seems so fitting."

The elderly woman nodded, a slight smile tugging at her lips. "It is, isn't it? Hannah was always the underdog champion. And I suppose, in some way, she saw Blue Squiggle Man as being the underdog in that threesome."

They laughed together for a few moments, the cloud of sadness that had hovered in the room lifting. When Genevieve finally spoke again, her voice was still sad but tinged with pride.

"Hannah was a wonderful little girl and an amazing woman. I feel blessed to have been the one God chose to be her mother."

NINETEEN

3:30 p.m.

HER HANDS FLEW ACROSS the keyboard as she wrote her article on Hannah Daltry. The initial news story about the woman's death had provided basic facts about the crime. But this story would be different, this story would bring a depth to the murder that few people would see any other way.

Spending the morning with Genevieve Daltry had been poignant. The woman's pain was visible in so many ways beyond the ever-present moisture in her eyes. Yet she'd been eager to share her daughter's life with Elise, the ups and downs that normal people face. People like Elise's readers.

The photo album and writing booklet that Hannah had assembled during her life showed a woman who treasured her childhood and the people in it—a woman who dreamed of being a writer at a very young age, saving her earliest work as a sort of snapshot from her journey. It was that same woman that Elise wanted to introduce to her readers as a reminder of just how senseless crime could be.

And not just for the victim of a murder. Seemingly lesser crimes impacted victims on so many levels. One only had to read Hannah Daltry's writing sample to know that.

Genevieve had granted permission to have her daughter's work published in the paper, but Elise hadn't decided if that was the route she would take just yet. Simply telling the story and using bits and pieces of the essay might be powerful enough. She'd have to wait and see as the story unfolded beneath her fingers.

She poised at the keyboard for a moment as her eyes scanned the paragraphs she'd written so far. It was coming together nicely. Thought-provoking but not sensational. A separate article would look at the original crime from the viewpoint of the Paleville Police Department as well as routine procedures followed by authorities when it came to protecting witnesses.

"So, when do I get to take the pictures?"

Elise pulled her gaze from the screen and looked up. Dean.

Her hands jumped from the keyboard to the top drawer of her desk, a preemptive strike against any rummaging the photographer might try. "Pictures?"

He pushed a strand of stringy blond hair out of his eye and picked at an imaginary piece of lint on his Kiss t-shirt. "You're not the brightest bulb in the box, are you, missy?"

"Wait." Elise carefully removed one hand from the front of the drawer and pressed "save" on her keyboard. "Okay. Pictures. The ones on my Hannah Daltry story, yes?"

Clapping filled the newsroom, prompting Tom and Karen to lean around their computer monitors to see what they were missing. Elise could feel her face warming as she waved them off.

"Yes. *Those* pictures," Dean said, yawning.

Elise moved her free hand from the keyboard to the information she had jotted down specifically for this reason. "Here. Hannah's mother—Genevieve Daltry—has agreed to allow you to visit. She has a photo album that Hannah had given her last Mother's Day as well as a booklet she'd put together as a child with her writing projects. I'd like you to get some sort of a shot with those. You'll know it when you see it."

Dean looked at the note she handed him and nodded. "Okay. What else?"

"The second notation on there pertains to the robbery from thirty-five years ago. I'm not sure how I'm going to play the writing sample Hannah wrote just yet, but I'd love it if you could illustrate the more vivid images of this piece for me." Elise handed him one of two copies she'd made of the teacher's work before leaving the assisted living facility that morning. "I leave the choice of *how* to illustrate it up to you. Just be aware that I'm not sure how I'll be using them at this point, if at all."

He nodded again then raised his right hand in mock salutation. "Yes, ma'am."

"Oh, and Dean?"

The photographer stopped mid bag-hoist and studied her. "What?"

"Try to refrain from adding Genevieve Daltry to your email barn okay? It is okay to find some friends of your own, you know."

"What are you talking about?"

Elise turned in her seat, her back pushed against her drawer. "What's with you sending email to Uncle Ken and Mitch's Aunt Betty? How'd you get their email addresses in the first place?"

He shifted foot to foot then began walking toward the front door, his words tossed over his shoulder like a pinch of salt. "I responded to that email you forwarded. I guess they liked my answers and emailed me in return. The rest is history."

Okay, that made sense. She shrugged to herself then spun back to the computer, her hands poised to begin typing once more. Only…

"Wait!"

She jumped up and headed in the direction Dean had gone, the front door shutting just as she reached Debbie's desk. Darn.

"He thinks I'm his personal slave or something. Next thing I know, he'll be bringing in his laundry for me to iron."

Elise eyed Debbie as she shoved a stack of Ocean Point postcards into the outgoing mail sack, the humor of her co-worker's words making her chuckle. "What are you talking about?"

"Dean. The guy can't even pop a few pieces of mail into the sack on his own." Debbie chewed her gum with vigor, her face contorted with irritation. "You try looking after him—you won't find him so funny. Trust me."

She held up her hands in surrender. "Oh, trust me. I wouldn't be wild about his demands either. But you've gotta admit that what you just said was funny."

Debbie stopped popping her gum and stared at her, dumbfounded. "What? What'd I say?"

It was even funnier as she recycled the words through her own mouth. "You said the next thing you knew Dean would be expecting you to iron his clothes. *Iron his clothes?* Think about it."

Seconds later, Karen and Tom were leaning around their computers once again. Only this time it wasn't Dean's clapping that interrupted their work. Debbie's snort-filled laughter echoed off the walls as she slapped her desk with her hand, tears rolling down her cheeks as she held her stomach.

"What's so funny?" Tom asked from behind his desk in the middle of the newsroom.

Debbie exhaled slowly, counted to ten silently with her fingers in an attempt to maintain enough composure to answer the sports reporter. A composure Elise was sorely lacking in the throes of her own shoulder-heaving. "Two words. *Dean.* And an *iron.*"

Karen's prissy voice emerged from behind her computer, "That, ladies, will be the day hell freezes over."

TWENTY

8:30 p.m.

HE REACHED FOR HER HAND as they left the theater, tucking it inside his own. They'd opted to walk the six blocks from Mia's to the movie house just so they could spend some more time together. With his current workload and her regular meetings and story assignments, they had barely spoken since dinner at Aunt Betty's on Sunday. He missed her.

Mitch looked over at Elise as they walked, his body warming as he watched the way her eyes crinkled when she talked. She was always so animated, so happy. She was good for him that way.

Letting go of her hand, he slipped his arm around her shoulder and pulled her close as they crossed the corner at Sand Castle and Ocean Wave. "So how'd it go with Doug the other day? He take care of you?"

"Detective Brunetti? Oh, he was great. Very nice, very giving of his time." Elise snuggled up against Mitch as they passed the dry cleaners and Leo's Pizzeria. "He was helpful with the general information I needed, but more importantly, he was able to fill in a lot for me in terms of Hannah's childhood and how the bank robbery may have affected her."

He loved listening to her talk about her stories. She always got so fired-up, so into whatever she was writing. The flip side, unfortunately, was the way the sad stuff seemed to eat away at her happiness. But he knew she wouldn't be the same Elise Jenkins if she didn't care. And he wouldn't trade the way she was for anything in the world.

They slowed as they came to Ocean Point Gifts, peering in the window at the new display of knick knacks and novelty items. Elise pointed to a framed photograph of the sun rising over the ocean. "Oh, Mitch, Uncle Ken would love that, wouldn't he?"

"Yeah, he would. It even looks like the kind of picture he'd take." He pulled her closer and planted a kiss on her head, closing his eyes as he inhaled her distinctly sweet, feminine scent. "Mmmmmm."

She tilted her head upward and moved her hands to his face. "What are you doing?"

"What do you think?" he asked, his voice raspy.

"I don't think you're looking at the stuff in the window anymore." She moved closer to him, her body curving to his.

"You are extremely observant, you know that?" He bent down and kissed her. "What gave me away?"

Elise tapped her index finger to her lip and scrunched her face. "Hmmm, I think it was the fact that you were looking at *me* more than the window."

"I never saw you turn your head."

"I never saw you turn yours either," she grinned. "But you've got a reflection too you know."

"Busted!" Turning her gently, he pointed at the window, their reflections peering back from the glow of the streetlight. "Look at yourself. I mean, really *look* at yourself. I'd be a blind imbecile not to spend my time looking at you rather than a bunch of sand dollar decorations."

The light falling across the sidewalk was just enough to see the red slip across her cheeks as she stood there, staring up at him. She was beautiful no matter what time of day, but there was something magical about her at that very moment. "Come on. Let's head back to the car."

As they walked, she shared more about her interview with Doug Brunetti, including his personal connection to the murder victim. "He actually pinpoints her behavior after the robbery as the driving force behind his becoming a police officer. He didn't like seeing her suffer like she did."

It was like that for a lot of the guys he worked with. So many of them—including himself—went into police work in the hopes they could make things better. On days when his biggest task was paperwork, he had to doubt whether he was doing a damn thing. But on days when he was able to bring solace to someone, it was everything he dreamed. Jonathan understood that feeling too…

Jonathan.

They crossed a side street and turned up Second

Street. "Hey, I had the strangest conversation with Jonathan earlier today."

Her sweet voice filled the quiet night air as she slipped her hand back into his. "Is he okay?"

"Oh yeah, he's fine. He called to give me some feedback from the kids' camp evaluations. It was all great. They really loved it." He guided her around a broken piece of sidewalk and pointed toward the car. "Anyway, he mentioned Dean."

"Dean?"

He laughed at her reaction which fell somewhere between surprise and frustration. "What's that for? You kinda sounded surprised and you kinda didn't."

She stopped in the middle of the sidewalk and groaned up at the stars. "He's been very weird since he got his computer. He asked me to forward on one of those goofy blanket mail things and I did." She stepped back a few feet and leaned against the hood of his car. "The next thing I know, he's in touch with Uncle Ken and Aunt Betty."

"Aunt Betty? *My* Aunt Betty?"

"Do you know another?" she quipped.

He looped his arm around her neck and pulled her close in a mock choke hold. "Smart aleck."

When he released her, she stepped back and threw her hands in the air. "I'm serious, though. First, Aunt Betty…then, Uncle Ken. And now *Jonathan*? What is he doing?"

"We're talking about Dean here, 'Lise, remember?

The guy isn't normal. Cool and fun, yes. Normal, no. We know this."

"True." The word was barely out of her mouth when the laughter started. Soft at first, growing louder and more contagious as she continued.

"What?" He felt his smile widening as she kept laughing, her shoulders getting into the act as well. "What'd I say?"

"No. Not. You." It was a struggle for her to speak between fits of laughter, so he simply folded his arms and waited. Just when he thought she'd stopped, she'd start again. But finally, she was able to speak. "It's just that today I was up at Debbie's desk and she was ranting and raving about him. He'd given her a handful of postcards to mail and she was irked he didn't just do it himself."

"O-kay…" He waved his hand in a circular motion, hoping she'd get to the part that had made her laugh so hard.

"I'm standing there watching her as she's stuffing the mail bag, complaining, and she goes something like, 'the next thing you know, he'll be asking me to iron his clothes.'" Elise began giggling again.

"Oh-kay."

"Mitch! How can you not see how funny that is? *Think*. What does Dean wear? Concert t-shirts. Everyday. What on earth would he have to iron?"

He cracked a smile and offered an agreeable shrug.

She waved her hand in the air and rolled her eyes at him. "Maybe you had to be there…but even Karen got it."

Now *that* was a surprise. Karen Smith was known around town as the ice princess. So, if the conversation about Dean had made *her* crack a smile, it must have been funnier in person. "Okay. I'll take your word for it."

He unlocked the passenger side and held the door open as Elise got in. "You know…Dean's lucky."

"Why's that?"

"Hang on a minute." Mitch shut her door and walked around the front of the car to his own side. "If he asked one of the ladies at *our* front desk to mail some postcards for him, they'd brain him with that new computer of his."

"Yeah. Debbie may be loud but she's fairly laid back when it comes to what everyone asks her to do. Postcards and…"

He glanced over at her as her voice trailed off in favor of a slight gasp. "What's wrong?"

She put a hand to her mouth and stared out the windshield without responding.

"Elise? What's wrong?" Turning in his seat, he touched her arm. "Baby?"

When she looked at him, her eyes were wide and frightened, her hand trembling in front of her mouth. "Dean."

Now he was confused. "What about Dean?"

"The new computer."

He waited, watching her face as the words slowly tumbled from her mouth."

"The postcards…"

Where was she going with this?

"The cheap watch…"

He straightened in his seat, her words starting to make sense. Computers, postcards, watches. Those were all items that had been lifted from Ocean Point over the past three weeks. But what did that have to do with Dean?

She grabbed his arm and gently shook it. "Don't you see? Dean shows up at a staff meeting last week with a new watch. Didn't really hit me until Sam pointed it out yesterday and teased him about its value."

He nodded, waiting for her to bring it home so he could understand what had her so upset.

"Then the computer. I mean, come on…Dean hates technology. Hates it. He still doesn't shoot digital. He's mocked me mercilessly for the past ten months about my need to check email twice a day. He swore he'd never buy a computer. And then he does."

The picture was coming into focus rapidly, the image disturbing at best.

"Today he pushes a bunch of postcards onto Debbie to mail. Let's be honest, who on earth does he have to mail postcards *to*?"

Mitch ran his hand across his face and through his hair, unsure of how to piece everything together. There was no doubt about it, something was fishy…but Dean?

"And after the last robb—" Elise sucked in her breath and paused briefly. "We had a staff meeting. He questioned me about you not being around to investigate the crimes. He was really weird about it, almost uncomfortable."

"Whoa. What'd he say? Exactly?" He gripped the

steering wheel with his left hand, his right holding steady across his face.

Elise leaned her head against the seatback and closed her eyes. "I don't know. Something like being surprised you'd go traipsing off while crimes were happening."

"Did he mention the victim?"

She shook her head. "No. We didn't know about Hannah's body being found until after that exchange took place." She paused for a moment, her voice growing so quiet he had to strain to hear her words. "At least the *rest* of us didn't know…"

TWENTY-ONE

12:30 p.m.
Wednesday, April 6

SHE'D INTENDED TO SPEND her lunch hour writing, but she simply needed to put a little distance between herself and the office. Or, rather, a little distance between herself and the likelihood of running into her co-worker.

Glancing down at her watch, she mentally calculated how long it would take Dean to drive to Paleville, take pictures at the assisted living facility and the bank, and drive back. Throw in a couple of food stops in both directions, and he should be arriving back at the newspaper within the next hour.

Mitch had said he'd call the office himself and leave a note with Debbie, requesting that Dean call him at his earliest convenience. And sure enough, when she left for lunch, a little pink sticky with Mitch's name and number was on Dean's clipboard behind the receptionist's desk.

She'd barely slept a wink all night, trying to come up with various plausible explanations for the similarity between Dean's newest possessions and the missing items around town. But every time she'd come up with one, her mind would immediately revert back to the robberies.

Please, please don't be Dean. Please.

The guy was annoying on a good day, but he'd become her friend. Someone she could count on to turn a bad mood around or to keep her on her toes. Like a brother in a way.

Please.

It had taken every ounce of her energy to keep from talking to Sam about her fears that morning. But Mitch had insisted, cautioning her to take it slow, let him do his job. The taking it slow part was the hardest of all. This wasn't just some person she knew from a distance. This was Dean. *Her* Dean.

Slowly she made her way down Second Street, by-passing all the places where she could stop and get a bite to eat. Her stomach was definitely twisting, but not from hunger…

She stopped outside Ocean Point Gifts, her eyes seeking out the framed photograph she'd admired the night before. The rising sun sparkling across the cresting waves was breathtakingly beautiful even with her heavy heart. She stared at it for a few moments, thinking and pondering, until her grandmother's voice whispered through her thoughts.

"Doing for others always brings peace to the giver."

Well, if there was ever a time to test that theory…

Elise tugged the shop door open and stepped inside, the breeze from the ocean jangling a nearby wind chime.

"Good afternoon. May we help you find something today?" A man of about fifty-five stepped out from behind the counter.

"There's a photograph in your window that I'd like to purchase. Do you ship items?"

"Yes. Yes, we do. And if the item is a gift, we can wrap it as well." He motioned for her to lead him to the picture, falling in step behind her.

"Gift wrap would be great, thanks." She picked up the frame and turned it, her gaze immediately riveted to the beauty of the shot once again. "This is it. It's just lovely."

Taking the frame from her hand, he led the way back to the counter. "It's taken by a local photographer here in Ocean Point."

A small wind chime topped with a smattering of sea-shells caught her eye as she passed by, prompting thoughts of Uncle Ken's fiancée, Sophie. Stopping, she lifted it carefully from its hook and checked the price. Twenty dollars. "I'd like to add this too."

"Of course." He took the wind chime from her hand and attached it to a hook at the counter. "Anyway, we loved this photographer's work so much we decided to take some of his shots on a consignment basis. If they sell as well as we hope, then we'll simply stock him on our own."

"Who's the photographer?" she asked as her hand twirled a rack of magnets to her left. A sand dollar with an ocean scene painted on its front caught her eye.

"Dean Waters."

Her hand dropped to her side as her mouth gaped open. "Dean Waters?"

"Yes, do you know him? He's the photographer for the local paper."

Feeling suddenly uncomfortable, she eked out a response. "Yes. We work together."

The man wrapped the frame in tissue paper and placed it in a gift box. "Oh really? What do you do at the paper?"

"I'm a reporter." She could hear the wooden sound to her voice and worked to soften it. "My name is Elise Jenkins."

"Ohhhhhhh, Elise." He sealed the box shut with a small disc-shaped gold sticker and extended his hand to her. "I'm Russ Walker. My wife, Gerty, runs the place but she's home with a cold today. She'll be disappointed she missed you. She's been hoping to meet you. She said you were very nice on the phone when you called to talk about the robbery."

"That's nice, thank you. I'm sure I'll be back again. I've avoided coming in the past ten months because I suspected you had too many lovely things in here for me to resist. And I was right." She forced her mind off Dean and onto her surroundings. "I'm sorry your store got robbed. I'm sure that was stressful."

The man nodded as he carefully removed the wind chime and placed it in a rectangular box. "It was. But we did okay. Didn't lose anything of any real value.

And, most importantly, no one was hurt." He sealed the box with a gold sticker and handed her a pad of paper. "Here, fill this out with the address we are shipping to, and we'll get it out in the mail this afternoon."

When she'd completed the information, she gave it to him and paid her bill, hoping against hope that her grandmother's oft-spoken words would prove true today.

"Thank you so much," she said, lifting her purse off the counter as she smiled at Russ. "I appreciate your help and it was very nice meeting you."

"It was nice meeting you too, young lady." He emerged from behind the counter and walked with her toward the front door. "Come see us any time."

She scanned the walls and shelves as she approached the door, noting a few little knick knacks that would look cute in her apartment, but it was the plaque on the wall that made her stop in her tracks.

Sierra McDermott smiled back at her from the center of the award, "Employee of the Year" engraved in a gold plate beneath.

"That's Sierra. Sierra McDermott. When did she work here?"

Russ stopped behind her and started counting under his breath. "Um, she started about two years ago, I think. Stayed with us here for about a year." He pointed at the picture as a look of pride flitted across his face. "That one was a helluva hard worker. We struck gold the day we snatched her from Merv. Then lost it ourselves when the bridal shop came knocking."

2:30 p.m.

No MATTER HOW MANY times she looked up from her computer, Dean still didn't materialize. And she was worried. The pink sticky with Mitch's call was no longer attached to his clipboard when she returned from the gift shop. A few beat-around-the-bush type questions yielded nothing from Debbie beyond the fact that the photographer had returned from Paleville only to leave again fifteen minutes later.

That was an hour ago.

Elise tried to focus on her article, to let Mitch do his job. But it was difficult. She hoped Mitch was right, that there would be some silly little explanation for Dean suddenly having a new computer, cheap watch, and a handful of postcards.

"Elise!"

She turned around in her chair at the sound of her name being whispered. From where she sat, she could see both Tom and Karen's terminals. The sports reporter was nowhere to be seen, his ball cap missing from atop his computer. Karen was there, but she was typing away with headphones strapped to her ears—listening to Mozart, no doubt.

"Elise!"

Debbie?

The thought disappeared from her mind as quickly as it came. Debbie didn't whisper. Ever. It was like Dean and an iron.

Standing up, she looked toward the receptionist's desk, shocked to see that hell had indeed frozen over. At least in the front half of the office.

The receptionist waved her over, her hands flapping at her side like a territorial goose. "Did you see him?" Debbie whispered.

Elise looked around the office again, her scan expanding to the waiting area and foyer as well. "See who?" She whispered back.

"Jacob Brown."

"Jacob Brown? Here? When?"

The territorial goose began strutting around her desk, mindful of the golden egg she had. "You sure you want to know? I mean, I don't want to interrupt your writing or anything."

"Tell me," she hissed.

Debbie plopped down in her seat and pulled a jar of nail polish from the top drawer of her desk. Slowly she uncapped it, leaning over the index finger on her right nail. "Chipped my polish a little while ago. I hate it when that happens."

Darn the luck…

"Debbie!"

"Okay, okay." Debbie brushed more polish on the offender and grinned up at Elise. "He asked to see Sam."

"Why?"

"I don't know. Asking that would make me nosey, don't you think?"

Elise laughed.

"Hey! I take offense to that. I may know a lot, but it's only because I'm observant."

She leaned against the half wall that separated her from the receptionist area and drummed her fingers on the top. "Okay. So what did you *observe* about him being here?"

"Better. Much better." Debbie lowered her voice again and periscoped her head over the counter, peering down the hallway that led to Sam's private office. "He had a paper in his hand."

"Paper...paper...paper," Elise mumbled under her breath. And then she remembered. Jacob's essay from class. Sam had said he'd love to publish it if Jacob would grant permission.

Baby steps...

"Pretty interesting, wouldn't you say?"

Maybe the ice was beginning to break...

"Woo-hoo, earth to Elise."

"Huh? What?" Startled, Elise looked at Debbie, realized the woman was talking to her despite the fact she'd heard nothing of the past few sentences. "I'm sorry. My thoughts ran away with me for a minute. No sign of Dean yet?"

"Nope." Debbie put her hand on the ringing phone. "What's the urgency about seeing Dean?"

"Nothing." Elise waved a retreat at the receptionist as she made her way down the hallway in the direction of the water fountain. Which, coincidentally, was just a few steps from Sam's office.

Snatches of muted conversation floated into the hallway from her boss's open door. The voices inside sounded amicable, a few chuckles dotting the air from time to time as added confirmation that things were okay.

She pushed the small circular button and put her mouth to the water, her ears still trained for any bits of conversation she could cull.

"Sierra is really the reason I took the class. She's been trying to refocus my attention and wanted to help get me going towards writing again."

Sam's calm voice wasn't far behind.

"It's always nice to have someone pushing your wagon from time to time. Makes reaching your destination even nicer when you know someone believed in you the whole way."

Elise straightened up, wiped excess water from her chin. Sam was right. That's exactly how she felt about Mitch. And Sam.

"I don't know what I did to get a girl like Sierra, but she's wonderful. Believes in me one hundred percent. She listens too. Sometimes I feel bad when I talk too much about my troubles, because she takes it all to heart. Like she's supposed to fix it all somehow."

Feeling suddenly guilty for eavesdropping on a conversation that was none of her business, Elise wandered back to the newsroom. She felt more content somehow, more at peace. Jacob Brown was a good kid who'd been dealt a tough blow in life. He'd be okay. His sharing his essay with her boss was a pretty big step.

She sat down at her desk, her gaze resting briefly on the blinking cursor halfway down her computer screen. The article on young victims—and how child psychologists work with them—was coming out well. But her mind was no longer on that story. Or *any* story, for that matter.

All she could think about at that moment was food. It didn't really matter what kind, just so long as it stopped the gurgling and pangs that had kicked up after her stop at the water fountain.

Her drawer, of course, held nothing. No pretzels. No back-up Caramello bar. No cookies. Nothing. Those would all be in Dean's stomach. Frustrated, she yanked open the zipper on her backpack purse and fished around inside, her hand closing on a package of cheese crackers she'd thrown in the other day.

As she pulled the rectangular package out, her purse tipped, spilling crinkled papers and loose change all over the floor. "Ugh!"

"Let me help."

Elise looked up, smiled at Tom. "Thanks."

They fumbled around on the ground until they had everything. When they were done, the sports reporter simply lifted the purse from the ground and set it on her desk. "That's not your lunch, is it?"

"Yeah. But it's my own fault. I went shopping during my lunch hour instead. I wanted to get something for my uncle."

Tom shifted his weight and cleared his throat softly. "His birthday?"

"Nope. Just because." Elise re-zipped her purse and ripped open the cracker package. "Want some?"

He held up his hand and shook his head. "That doesn't surprise me."

She swallowed her first mouthful of cracker. "What doesn't?"

"That you'd use your break time to do something nice for someone. It's very you." Tom patted her arm and turned toward his computer, bending quickly. "Oh wait, I think this is yours too."

The receipt was from Ocean Point Gifts for a wind chime and a picture frame. "Oh yeah, thanks."

The remaining five crackers went quickly as she looked at the receipt on her desk and mentally walked through the gift shop again. The magnets were cute. And so were the Ocean Point novelty items. She closed her eyes as the rumbling in her stomach began to subside, her thoughts on the wind chime she hadn't planned on buying. But Sophie would love it.

And Sierra's picture. That was a surprise.

Snatched from Merv's to work at Ocean Point Gifts...

Her eyes flew open and she sat up straight, a troubling thought suddenly plaguing her mind. Merv's? Ocean Point Gifts? A former employee of the first two robbery locations, a student at the third?

No. No way.

Nibbling on her lower lip, Elise forced her attention back to the screen in front of her, to the place in the article where she had stopped. But it was no use. If she could suspect Dean, then—

"Oh my God!"

"Talking to yourself now? That's not a good sign, missy."

Elise looked up, her eyes widening at the sight of the photographer standing beside her desk with his camera bag on his shoulder, a playful grin on his face. "What?"

"You're talking to yourself. You just said, 'Oh my God.'" Dean reached across her body and picked up the empty cracker wrapper. "Hey!"

"Where did you get your computer?"

He lifted the wrapper to his nose and sniffed. "Hey, these are my favorites!"

She grabbed his arm. "I'm serious, Dean, please. Where'd you get your computer?"

"What's all this fascination with my computer? First Mitch, then you."

"Dean!"

"Okay, okay." He slid his bag from his shoulder and set it on her desk. "But I already told you."

She searched her memory bank for the conversation he was referring to. "No you didn't."

"Yeah, I did. You asked me about her. Actually, let me rephrase that. You *hounded* me about her."

"I hounded you? How? When? About who…"

And then she knew. Sierra.

Scrambling to keep some semblance of order to the millions of thoughts racing through her mind, she grasped Dean's arm tighter. "You said she was helping you. You didn't say you *bought* it from her."

"Well, duh, do you really think I'd bring a computer to Mia's without knowing how to turn it on? Sheesh. What do you think I am, stupid? Wait, don't answer that. Anyway, I heard through the grapevine that she had an extra computer she was willing to unload for a hundred bucks. I couldn't resist." He pried her hand from his arm and opened her drawer, shutting it seconds later in disgust. "You really must go shopping, missy. And where did you have those crackers stashed in the first place? They weren't in your drawer three hours ago."

She let it pass. There'd be plenty of time to smack him for rummaging without permission. Again.

"So you'd just bought it that night?"

"Bingo! Give the chick a prize, ladies and gentlemen!" Dean spread his arms and bellowed into the air.

"Pipe down, Dean! I'm trying to work!"

His jaw slacked open. "Did Debbie—aka Megaphone Mouth—just tell *me* to pipe down?"

"And those postcards you mailed the other day? Where'd you get those?"

Dean stared at her. "Huh?"

"Yesterday, you asked Debbie to mail some postcards for you. Where'd you get them?"

"Damn it, can't that woman ever keep her mouth shut?" he said, turning on his heel and heading toward the reception area.

"Dean, wait, please!"

He turned. "What?"

"The postcards, where'd you get them?" she pleaded.

"The bag." Dean slapped the heel of his hand to his forehead and theatrically stumbled around. "Women."

The bag...the bag...

"What bag, Dean?"

A noise resembling a frustrated moan rolled from his mouth as he banged his head against the wall. "The *bag*, Elise. The *computer* bag."

TWENTY-TWO

4:00 p.m.

THINK, ELISE. THINK.

It was a mantra that was on continuous playback in her mind. The words cautioned her to slow down, process the information she'd strung together over the past hour or so.

But it was hard. Particularly when the pieces fit as well as they did.

The question now was what to do. Did she call Mitch and share her fears with him? Or did she see if she could gleam even more information before hassling him at work?

She opted for more.

First, the essay. All of a sudden Sierra's assignment seemed more personal than it had when she'd read it to the class on Saturday. It had drawn Elise in at the time, made her imagine the story that was being shaped. Yet now, it didn't seem like a story in the making any longer.

She found Sam at his desk, his back to the door as he flipped through last week's paper.

"Sam? Can I talk to you for a minute?"

He swiveled around in his desk and motioned her inside. "Of course. What can I do for you?"

She waved off his invitation to sit, stopping, instead, to the side of his desk. "Do you happen to have everyone's assignments from last week's class? The ones we read aloud?"

"Yeah, I do." His eyebrows arched upward. "What's wrong?"

"I need to see Sierra's." She wiped her moist palms against her slacks, aware of the way Sam was studying her face. "Please. It's important."

He spun around in his chair and unzipped the black briefcase to the left of his computer monitor. "They should all be in here. Funny you ask about them. Jacob Brown was in earlier, with an extra copy of his story and his signed permission at the bottom. He wants me to run his essay. I told him we'd do it in conjunction with the story you're working on now—the one about the survivors of crime and how it affects them."

She nodded her agreement, her eyes watching his every move as he sorted through the pile of essays in his case. "Yeah, sure, okay."

"What's wrong?" Sam pulled Sierra's essay from the pile and spun back toward Elise, his whole face giving way to worry.

"I think I may have figured out who's behind the robberies." She slid the essay from her boss's outstretched hand, her eyes flying down the words on the page.

It was not what it seemed.

But how could he tell?

All he'd meant to do was help. To make things better.

Yet somehow it went horribly wrong. What was supposed to be better was now worse. What was supposed to help, hurt more.

He cowered in a corner, alone, eyeing his mistakes from afar. Desperate to fix things, unsure of how—or if—it could be done.

Seeking help would bring an end. Ignoring it could bring a loss much greater and provide an unjust freedom.

It was not what it seemed.

But how could he tell?

It was too much. The words seemed almost Greek. She needed help.

Dropping into the empty chair, Elise poured everything out as Sam listened quietly. She explained how she'd suspected Dean at first, how that morphed into a gut feeling about Sierra.

She looked down at the page as she continued. "I mean, if you change the pronoun to "she" it could make sense. She had familiarity with all three locations. She'd be afraid to tell because of the punishment…but why? Why would she do it?"

"Well, let's try to think what could be accomplished from a crime like this. She obviously didn't need the stuff she stole, or she wouldn't sell it to Dean for…what?"

"A hundred dollars," she said, not looking up.

"A hundred bucks," Sam repeated. "We know those computers are worth ten times that. At least. So money wasn't the motive."

All he'd meant to do was help. To make things better.

That line bothered her. How would robbery make things better? She posed the question to Sam.

"I don't know. What does a robbery do? It gets a person some money or some objects…it gets attention…it—"

"That's it!" Elise jumped from her seat, her hand gripping the essay tightly. "Oh my gosh…it makes sense!"

"You lost me."

"Sam, don't you see? It's like Mitch's aunt said the other night. The robberies gave the news reporters something else to focus on. It brought talk of the fortune teller murders to a halt for a little while. Only…"

"Only what?" Sam asked, his voice rising with excitement.

"Only it backfired. When Hannah was murdered, the television reporters were right back to talking about last year." Elise paced back and forth as she spoke, her mind running various scenarios. "But I can't see Sierra hurting a flea let alone murdering an innocent woman. Taking a few minor objects to help Jacob, maybe. Killing someone, no way."

"Shhh." Sam stood up, walked around the desk and raised Elise's hand so he could reread Sierra's essay himself. "Look right here." He pointed to the fourth paragraph.

Yet somehow it went horribly wrong. What was supposed to be better was now worse. What was supposed to help hurt more.

She nodded, her eyes moving further down the page.

Seeking help would bring an end. Ignoring it could bring a loss much greater and provide an unjust freedom.
   It was not what it seemed.
   But how could he tell?

"Wait a minute!" Her heart rate accelerated as a thought took hold above all others. "Maybe the murder isn't related to the robbery. She says it wasn't what it seemed. But seeking help would bring an end."

"An end in many ways for her," Sam chimed in.

"And for her relationship with Jacob." Elise stared at the words, rereading them over and over again aloud. "Ignoring it could bring a loss much greater and provide an unjust freedom…ignoring it could bring a loss much greater and provide an unjust freedom…"

"By not admitting her part in the robberies, the

person responsible for Hannah Daltry's death gets off scot-free," Sam mumbled.

That was it. It all made sense now.

"There's still one more thing I need to check first. May I use your phone?"

"Absolutely. Sam walked around his desk and pushed the phone in her direction. "Go ahead."

She knew the number by heart. But it didn't make the call any easier.

"Detective Burns, please. It's Elise Jenkins."

Within seconds Mitch's warm voice filled her ear. "Hey, 'Lise. I talked to Dean and—"

"Mitch, I have to ask you something." She gripped the receiver and closed her eyes, her heart pounding so loudly she could hear it in her ears.

"O-kay. Shoot."

"How did the suspect get into the places he—or she—robbed?"

"Why?"

"Please, Mitch, just answer me."

"We're not sure. But we know there was no forced entry."

Her mind scrambled the information. "And that would be the case if the suspect had keys, right?"

There was silence in her ear for a moment.

"Mitch?"

"Yeah, I'm still here. Absolutely. But he'd have needed keys to both places."

It was confirmation she expected but didn't enjoy hearing. "And what about the college? That too?"

"No. That building was open anyway, so students could use the computers when needed. It gets locked after ten. But what's this about, Elise? What's going on?"

She inhaled deeply, the enormity of what she was about to say more than she could grasp at that moment. By figuring out the Sierra connection, the murder of Hannah Daltry took on a whole new significance.

TWENTY-THREE

8:30 p.m.

IT WAS LIKE MEETING all your deadlines, yet knowing it started all over again on Monday morning. From scratch.

She'd been right about Sierra. And she'd been right about Hannah. Neither made her feel any better about telling Mitch.

Sure, there was a much better chance of finding the teacher's murderer now that they knew where *not* to look, but that realization had come with a price tag. Sierra McDermott was now facing prosecution for something she did out of love for someone else. The act was wrong, her motives pure.

Glancing down at her cell phone, she gave in to her curiosity and dialed Mitch's number. He answered on the second ring.

"Hey, 'Lise. How are you holding up?"

The sound of his voice was the hug she'd been craving all evening. "I'm okay. How's Sierra?"

"Rattled. Upset. Apologetic. Scared."

"Makes sense." Elise wandered over to her living room window and peered outside. "Is she going to go to jail?"

"I don't know. I hope not." He sighed, frustration evident in his words. "I mean, what she did was wrong. But I can kind of see why she did it. She really loves Jacob."

Elise rested the side of her head on the window frame. "How is Jacob holding up? Sam called him and told him what was about to happen."

"The kid's okay. He's standing by Sierra, holding her hand. I think knowing just how much she loved him has really hit home for the guy, you know?"

"Yeah," she whispered. "I bet he's going to hate me even more now, huh?"

"No. Actually not at all. I think Sam told him how hard it was for you to do this, but that it had to come out so we can find Hannah Daltry's killer."

She stared, unseeingly, out at the pavement below. "I hope so, I really do. I didn't want to hurt Sierra or Jacob. Please know that."

"Aww, baby, of course I know that. You did the right thing." His voice lowered an octave. "I'm gonna come over and see you as soon as I'm done with all this paperwork and I make sure Sierra is okay."

"No!" She shook her thoughts into the present. "Please stay there and check on her. She's going to be so frightened in a cell overnight. I'm fine. Really."

"You sure?" he asked.

"Yeah." She couldn't tell him how badly she needed his arms, how strongly she wanted to be held. Because if she did, he'd come, and Sierra needed him more.

When they hung up, she grabbed Hannah's writing sample and headed for her bedroom. Sleep was a long way off but her bed was where she felt most cozy, most safe. An aura she desperately needed at that moment.

All evening she'd been plagued by thoughts of her teacher, trying desperately to figure out who would want to kill such a kind, creative woman. It simply made no sense.

Slipping out of her sweater and slacks, she stepped into a silky ocean-blue nightgown and climbed under the covers, propping two pillows under her head so she could read.

Once again her eyes were drawn to her teacher's account of that robbery so long ago. She couldn't help but wonder if the killer's identity had been shielded by a mask too. A series of questions tugging at her thoughts—did the masks make it easier to find closure, or did it make it harder?

And closure was the wrong term. It was obvious from talking to Detective Brunetti and Genevieve Daltry, and from Hannah's own words, that closure never truly came. Was that because there were no faces to direct anger toward?

She made a mental note of the question, realizing the answer was worthy of a follow-up call to the child psychologist she was using in her article on young crime victims.

The doctor had read Hannah's essay, commenting on

the way the seven-year-old had made associations. By doing that, she was breaking the horror down into manageable chunks.

Work boots like Daddy's...One of the bad guys being scared just like she was...Wearing a mask and gloves like a cousin...Gunshots sounding like fireworks...Blue Squiggle Man tripping over his shoe laces like she did...Pushing off the ground with grunts like her grandfather...

Leaning back against the pillows, she blew a puff of air out, a strand of her wavy hair flying upward momentarily. It was so frustrating and heartbreaking all at the same time. Frustrating, because she couldn't imagine who would want to kill her teacher. Heartbreaking, because the woman had endured so much fear in her life—almost as if fate had marked her as a victim.

She looked down at the page, her eyes riveted on the countless associations made by the little girl.

I knew I shouldn't stare, Mommy says it's not polite, but he reminded me of that girl, Sara, in the other second grade room. Maybe that's why he hung out with bosses. Because he didn't feel good about himself.

It was the one association she didn't get. Why did Blue Squiggle Man remind her of a classmate? And what did she mean about that being why he didn't feel good about himself?

She reread the paragraph four times in an effort to figure it out, but it was no use.

But maybe—

Raising up on her elbow, she leaned over the side of her bed and grabbed the yellow daisy-shaped wire basket on the nightstand. It was her catch-all bucket— the spot where things went after she emptied her pockets at night. She rummaged through the top layer or two until she found the cream-colored card.

Detective Douglas Brunetti
Paleville Police Department

He'd written his home number on the back before she'd left his office. His invitation to call anytime had seemed sincere. She'd know soon enough if that were true.

"Brunetti."

The comforter slipped from her shoulders as she sat up. "Detective Brunetti, this is Elise Jenkins."

She hoped the silence meant he was trying to place her name, not that he'd hung up. Fortunately, the silence was short-lived as his voice took on a friendly, more welcoming tone.

"Yeah, hi there, Elise. I'm glad you called. I stopped by to see Mrs. Daltry the other day and she sang your praises. Thank you for being so gentle with her."

She felt her face warm at his words. "It was easy. She's a neat woman."

"So what can I do for you? Did you come up with more questions for me?"

Her eyes immediately jumped to the essay lying across her lap. "Actually, I have one. Did you know a little girl named Sara? She would have been in the same grade level as Hannah when the robbery took place."

"Sara…no last name?"

"No. I'm sorry. That's all I've got."

"Hmmmm…." A tapping noise replaced talking as Detective Brunetti grew quiet. "Wait a minute, hang on, I'll be right back."

Pulling the comforter back to her shoulders, Elise sunk against the pillow. She was anxious for whatever information the detective could share, but it was hard not to follow the other trail of thoughts running through her mind. The trail that led to a scared girl alone in a cell.

She closed her eyes and willed herself to focus on the quiet in her ear. There was nothing she could do for Sierra now.

"Okay, Elise, I'm back. This is one time in life when being a pack-rat comes in handy. I've got yearbooks from grammar school. I looked up the second graders from thirty-five years ago. And guess what?"

She sat up. "What?"

"There's a Sara in the other classroom. Sara James."

"That's awesome, thank you so much, Detective Brunetti." Elise swung her feet out from under the covers and stepped onto the floor. "Any chance she still lives in Paleville?"

"Already looking that up."

"How'd you know?"

"Detectives, reporters…"

She laughed.

"Here we go. There's a Sara James at 52 Huntington Way."

Elise grabbed a notebook off her dresser and jotted down the address.

"And, because I know you'll ask, the phone number is 555-4246."

TWENTY-FOUR

11:00 a.m.
Thursday, April 7

FOR THE THIRD TIME in four days, Elise wound her way through the streets of Paleville, New Jersey. Only this time she was more apprehensive—unsure of what, exactly, she was hoping to learn from Sara James.

She glanced down at the address in her hand, then back up at the mailboxes she passed. Forty-six…Forty-eight…Fifty…Fifty-two.

"Here we are," she mumbled to herself as she pulled to a stop at the curb. The two-story Victorian home was in need of a handyman. Several of the second-floor shutters were cock-eyed, the eaves in desperate need of a few coats of paint. But what was lacking in structural maintenance was more than made up for by the landscaping and welcoming atmosphere of the wraparound front porch.

It wasn't hard to imagine the home during its heyday with children playing in the yard, adults sipping lemonade and swapping gossip on the front porch. In fact, the whole neighborhood hinted at a history ripe with warmth and friendship—collective celebrations for new babies and birthdays, shared sorrow over deaths and lost jobs, secrets told in confidence between the closest of friends.

She wondered if that was still the case here or if the present-day occupants of Huntington Way simply closed their doors at night, anxious to retreat into a world of their own. More importantly, though, where did Sara James fall on that spectrum? Would the woman be open to Elise's questions—if, in fact, she actually *had* some?

All morning she'd been eager to make this visit, hoping against hope that Sara James would be the missing puzzle piece. The only problem was the puzzle itself. What exactly did she hope to discover by talking to a young girl that had been in the same school as Hannah Daltry so many years ago?

She had no idea, frankly. But, for whatever reason, that didn't seem to matter. Her mind was set on talking to this woman.

Softly, Elise knocked on Sara's front door, her hands moistening as she waited. Seconds turned to minutes before the door finally opened and she was face-to-face with a woman of about five-foot-six with long brown hair and big hazel eyes. Her lips could only be described as a cupid's bow…if you could look past the extensive scarring that haloed the left side of her mouth and neck.

"Yes?"

"Sara James?"

Surprised, the woman nodded. "That's right. Can I help you?"

Trying not to stare, Elise extended her hand. "I hope so. My name is Elise Jenkins and I'm a reporter with the *Ocean Point Weekly*. I know I should have called first, but I was in the area and—"

The woman's eyes traveled slowly down Elise's mint green sweater and khaki trousers before returning to her face. "I don't understand."

Elise retracted her hand and rushed to explain. "I've been working on an article about a Paleville woman who was murdered in Ocean Point last week."

"Hannah…"

"Yes, Hannah Daltry. Did you know her?"

Stepping out from behind the door, the woman motioned to one of two rockers on the front porch. "Would you like to sit for a moment?"

"Yes, please." Elise selected the chair furthest from the door, perching on the edge as she met Sara's eyes. "Thank you for talking to me."

Sara laced her fingers together and set them on her lap. "I don't really understand why you're here or how you think I can help you with a story about Hannah Daltry."

A strong believer in the straight-forward approach, Elise opened up about her research into the victim's background. "Ms. Daltry's death impacted me personally. She was my creative writing teacher at Ocean Point Community College."

"That doesn't surprise me," Sara offered. "She was

always writing little stories in class and in scouts. It was as much *her* passion, as drawing was for *me*."

Elise unzipped her backpack purse and pulled out her notebook. "Would it be okay with you if I jotted notes while we talk?"

The woman shrugged. "I suppose, though I still don't understand why you're talking to me. There are others in this town that probably knew the Daltry family better than I did. Hannah and I were occasionally in class together during elementary school, but that was really it."

"What years were you in class together?"

Closing her eyes, Sara's lips moved as she talked through her answer. "I think third grade was the first time we were together. I knew who she was before that because she'd smile at me once in a while on the playground. That wasn't something I saw often."

"What do you mean?" Elise asked.

"Look at my face." Sara waved her left hand over the discolored skin beside her mouth and down her neck. "It didn't exactly attract friends as you can probably imagine."

"Kids can be so cruel." It was all she could think to say under the circumstances, but it still didn't seem to be enough.

"Yes, they can be. But not Hannah. I moved here just before second grade and it was so hard to make friends. They just saw me as this scary little kid because I looked different. My mom kept telling me to give it time…that they'd fall in love with who I was on the inside as they got to know me."

Elise felt her heart twist. "Sounds like good advice."

Sara smoothed a few wrinkles from her slacks before crossing her legs. "In theory, sure. But most kids didn't stick around long enough to see past the scars."

"I'm sorry," she whispered.

"Don't be. It's just my skin that's different. Not me. It took a lot of years to accept that, but I have. Gentle souls, like Hannah, that I ran into during my school career made the journey easier."

Elise looked down at her empty notepad, realizing she was listening with her heart more than her ears. "So Hannah was your friend?"

"No, I wouldn't say that. I'd say she noticed me…*saw* me. But by the time third grade rolled around, she seemed withdrawn. At first I thought I'd imagined the smiles on the playground the year before, but then I realized she was like that with everyone—teachers, other kids, the principal."

"She'd been through a lot too. Though, unlike your scars, hers were on the inside." Elise could feel her voice trembling as she spoke, her infamous sensitive side kicking into full gear.

Sara's lip began to tremble ever so slightly. "I'm so sorry to hear that. I wish I'd known. Maybe I could have helped somehow."

Reaching across her lap, Elise gently squeezed Sara's hand. "She worked through her own pain by writing."

"I understand that," Sara said softly. "I worked through mine by drawing."

"I'm glad. Thank you so much for talking to me." Elise stood and shook the woman's hand. "It's a shame the two of you hadn't found each other before... well...it's just a shame."

When she was finally in the car once again, Elise leaned back against the head rest and closed her eyes, her mind rewinding through her visit with Sara James. The woman's sadness over a painful childhood had been evident, breaking Elise's heart in the process.

"I wish I'd known. Maybe I could have helped somehow."

The woman's words echoed in her mind, filtered through the troublesome thoughts that nagged at her subconscious.

"What is wrong with me?" she asked aloud to no one but the clock radio and a steering wheel.

She reached for the paper on the passenger seat, unfolding it slowly as she gazed up at the house from which she'd just come. When it was open, she looked down at the familiar piece, at the words she'd studied countless times over the past two weeks. Her eyes fell on the paragraph she'd underlined in bed the night before.

I knew I shouldn't stare, Mommy says it's not polite, but he reminded me of that girl Sara, in the other second grade room. Maybe that's why he hung out with bosses. Because he didn't feel good about himself.

That was it! The final question was finally answered. Just like Work Boot Guys wore shoes like her Daddy, Blue Squiggle Man must have had a disfigurement that reminded her of Sara.

Too bad it wasn't enough to identify the man.

TWENTY-FIVE

8:00 a.m.
Friday, April 8

MEETING MADELYN CONNER for coffee, with just forty-five minutes to spare, was a risky move. On one hand, she should try to get in the habit of eating something before work anyway. But on the other hand, Madelyn liked to talk. And talk. And talk. And talk.

Elise smiled at the hostess and pointed at the slightly plump woman waving eagerly from a booth at the back of the diner. "I'm with her. Thanks."

"No problem, sugar. Fran will be over to get your order in a few minutes."

The Ocean Point Diner was a hot bevy of excitement on most mornings—the breakfast-spot-of-choice for the majority of retirees in town. The lunch crowd was primarily comprised of the local work force, catering to everyone from linemen to attorneys and everyone in between. The dinner crowd was anyone's guess with families and singles taking over the place in fairly equal proportions.

Her favorite part? The people-watching.

"Hey there, Elise, what's shaking?" Fran, a longtime waitress and customer-favorite, blew a quick bubble with her pink gum, withdrawing it quickly after the snap. "It's been slow in here today—nobody too special yet."

Elise and Fran had struck up a casual friendship last summer when she'd been interviewing a subject for a news article. The interview had been conducted over lunch at the diner and had been preceded by people-watching tips from Fran herself. They'd gotten along famously ever since.

"The morning's still young," Elise shot back as she made her way over to Madelyn's booth. When she reached the table, she took off her coat and folded it neatly on the seat. "Hi, Madelyn, how are you?"

"Wonderful! I'm so excited about meeting for coffee today. Have you been working on our latest assignment? How far have you gotten? Anything new on the Daltry murder?"

Elise grinned at her companion across the table, amused by the woman's ability to spew questions faster than she ever could. "You should have been a reporter, Madelyn. You're quick with the questions."

Madelyn's face flushed. "Sorry. But you're not the first one to say that. My dad used to say I should have been a reporter, or a trial attorney. Oh! And he mentioned an interrogator once too."

Ah. An interrogator. Perfect.

Fran appeared beside their table, notebook in hand. "What can I get you, ladies?"

Madelyn looked down at her menu. "The Farmer's special? Do the home fries have a seasoning of any kind?"

Fran tapped her chin with her pencil. "Hmmm, a little. Nothing too overpowering, though."

"Okay. And the French toast…does the cook use vanilla?"

Fran stopped tapping, slid her eyes in Elise's direction, then looked back at Madelyn. "I'm fairly certain he does, yes."

"And one more quick one. Your pancakes. Do you have a wheat version?"

"Yup."

Elise nibbled her lower lip inward to keep from laughing. If there was one person who couldn't look the other way when it came to Madelyn's endless talking, it would be Fran.

Madelyn inhaled sharply and set her menu down in front of Fran. "I'll just take a coffee. Black."

Fran's pencil-holding hand clenched into a fist and began moving in Madelyn's direction. In an effort to save one friend from losing her job and another from certain bruising, she stamped down her urge to forgo food and placed an order.

"I'll take a hot chocolate and a side order of wheat toast and bacon."

The waitress's hand continued its forward motion.

"Fran!"

"Huh?" The redhead shook her head furiously and

pulled her arm back to her notebook. "Sorry. Overcome by a desire to throttle for an instant."

"Oh, dear, I can only imagine the difficult customers you must get in here on a daily basis. You have my sympathies," Madelyn offered sympathetically.

Fran stared. Elise giggled.

When she managed to pull her jaw up off the ground, the waitress leaned her mouth close to Elise's. "You've got the best seat in the house this morning, kiddo."

While she could offer no argument, she had to admit she enjoyed Madelyn. Sure, the woman was overly talkative and a bit extreme in her enthusiasm over things, but she was sweet. And lovable.

Alone again, Madelyn leaned across the table and grasped Elise's hands. "So what's new in the investigation? I've been watching the news every night and they've got nothing different to say. Knowing what kind of a reporter *you* are, I figure you're more on top of things."

She was flattered by Madelyn's faith in her abilities, she really was. But she didn't feel comfortable sharing Sierra's role in the recent rash of robberies. The girl had enough on her plate right now; she didn't need news of her mistakes broadcast throughout town before it had to be.

And, with any luck, that time would never come if Mitch's prediction over the telephone that morning came to fruition. Russ and Gerty Walker at Ocean Point Gifts had declined to press charges against Sierra. Merv had dropped the charges as well. Both employers had been open-minded enough to listen to the story and recall their fondness for the suspect.

Now the only one the department was waiting to hear from was the community college. If they dropped the robbery charges as well, Sierra would be okay. If they didn't, she could potentially serve some jail time.

Elise looked around the diner, desperate for a way to redirect Madelyn's attention so she wouldn't have to come right out and lie to the woman. But there was nothing that jumped out at her—

Jacob.

The young man was seated on a stool in the counter section of the diner, his head bent low, his shoulders slumped. A plate, brimming with food, went unnoticed as he stared at nothing in particular. Her heart ached for him as she noted the sadness in his face. First his dad and now Sierra. It just didn't seem fair.

"Lookie here, Paul, the two prettiest women in the place are seated at the same table. Must be our lucky day."

"Oh, Al," Madelyn giggled.

Elise pulled her gaze off Jacob and trained it on the two men standing beside their booth.

"Hi, Al. Hi, Paul. It's nice to see you. How are you?" Elise looked from Al's happy face to Paul's impassive one. The men were nothing short of Felix and Oscar. Or, better yet, Frick and Frack. "I didn't know you were joining us."

"I didn't know either," Madelyn said, her face reddening as she dropped her eyes to the table.

Al lifted his ball cap off his head for a moment so he could push a few stray hairs off his forehead. When he was done, he pulled his cap back into place. "We didn't either. We just stopped in for a little coffee-to-go before our tee time," he raised his left hand slightly to indicate his golf glove, then lowered it back to his side, "I looked around, saw you two ladies and decided to stop over."

"We're glad you did." Elise scooted over on the vinyl bench and patted the spot next to her. "Can you sit for a little while?"

The added conversation would surely help get Madelyn's mind off the investigation. Or, at the very least, would distract her long enough that Elise would be able to beg off answering in favor of getting to the office in time.

"We'd love to, but we've got to go." Al raised his left arm again, pulling his coat sleeve back to afford visual access to his wristwatch. "We tee off in…twenty minutes."

Elise slapped a hand over her mouth to stifle a gasp as she stared at Al's arm above the glove line—the scars from his third-degree burn impossible to miss.

In that instant, everything that had eluded her about Hannah Daltry's death suddenly made perfect sense. The teacher *could* identify the third robber. She'd remembered—and written about—a detail that she'd associated with a classmate named Sara. A detail that the robber would realize could land him in jail for the rest of his life.

Unless, of course, he eliminated the one person who could put him there.

Hannah Daltry.

She hated to believe that the funny man who'd made her laugh so many times could take another person's life. But if she'd learned one thing from the fortune-teller murders and her trip to Mackinac Island, it was the fact that seemingly friendly people could change in an instant if it suited their needs.

"Is there something wrong, Elise?" Al asked as he stared at her. "You look like you saw a ghost just now when I looked at my watch."

"No, I—" She searched her mind for an excuse she could offer that would get her away from the table and in a place where she could call Mitch. "It's just—uh—well, I just remembered an interview I was supposed to do at 8:45 and I'm going to be late if I don't leave right now."

Madelyn's head whipped upward. "Oh, no, Elise. I was looking forward to our talk."

Elise reached a shaking hand across the table and patted Madelyn's arm. "I'm sorry. It's…what I get for not checking my calendar when you called. Rain check? My treat?"

The woman's shoulders relaxed, a smile replacing her frown. "Okay. Sure. Tomorrow? Before class?"

"Before class…" She could hear the disinterest in her voice, could feel Al's eyes pinning hers. "Um. Yeah. Before class. Sure."

Grabbing her coat and purse, Elise slid out from behind the booth and slapped a ten-dollar bill down on the table. "That's for Fran. Please offer my apologies when she returns with my food. I gotta go."

She tried to walk toward the door as casually as possible, but it was no use. As soon as she cleared Al and Paul's vicinity, she took off in a sprint, nearly knocking Jacob Brown from his feet as he stepped off his stool.

SHE FLIPPED OPEN her cell phone as she walked, her feet barely hitting the ground as she cut through a series of vacant lots between Beachside Bakery and an empty storefront off Second Street. Bypassing the sidewalk would shave valuable seconds off her time in getting to the office.

"Detective Burns, please."

"Elise?"

"Mindy, I need to talk to Mitch. It's super important."

"He just stepped out. Said he was heading over to your office with some news about Sierra McDermott."

"Thanks." Elise snapped the phone shut and quickened her pace, her heart racing a-mile-a-minute with the discovery of Hannah's murderer. It all fit so perfectly now. Everything down to the timing.

Less than forty-eight hours after handing out copies of her writing sample, Hannah Daltry was dead, her words striking awe and respect in everyone who read them. Except one.

For Al Nedley, Hannah's words struck something very different.

"Stop right there!"

Whirling around, Elise felt her stomach drop at the sight of Hannah's killer. "Hi, Al, I thought you were going golfing."

She tried to make her voice sound casual, upbeat, but she failed miserably and she knew it as well as he did.

"I can't let you tell." The man pulled his ball cap from his head and tossed it on the pavement at his feet, his fists clenching and unclenching at his side. "I was forced to stay away for nearly thirty-five years. But I can't stay away any longer. This is my home."

"I don't know what you're talking about," she squeaked, her feet slowly moving backward.

"Elise, I'm not stupid. And neither are you. When I read that writing sample she wrote, I was floored. I had no idea that kid had been there—none. But once I did, I knew it was only a matter of time before she put two and two together. Her memory was too vivid. So I did what I had to do. Those robberies? They're just my ticket to freedom in all this."

A sudden movement behind Al caught her eye and she tried not to react. If she did...if she so much as blinked...one of them was bound to get hurt.

"Your ticket to freedom?"

Al spun around and faced Jacob. Elise waved her arms behind Al's head, desperately trying to wave Jacob off. When he didn't listen, she screamed. "Run, Jacob! Get out of here!"

"There's no way I'm going to let a scumbag like this get away with murder."

Elise flipped her phone open and dialed her office. Debbie's voice filled her ear.

"Good morning, *Ocean Point Weekl—*"

"Is Mitch there?"

"Good morning to you too, Elise. As a matter of fact he—"

"Tell him to get over to the vacant lots next to the bakery. Tell him it's an emergency. I found Hannah's killer." She snapped the phone shut, eyed her elderly nemesis, and took off in a run, jumping on Al's back with all her weight.

The man groaned as she landed, rearing backward as Jacob kicked him in the gut, dropping him to his knees.

"This is my way of apologizing for being such a jerk to you the past few weeks," Jacob huffed as he bent his knee and drove it into Al's back. "I'm really sorry, Elise."

"How'd you know I was in trouble?" she asked, panting.

"I didn't. But I figured *something* was up when you nearly knocked me over on your way out of the diner." He shifted his weight from his knee, bringing his entire body onto Al's back. "So, since I wanted to apologize for my attitude anyway, I figured I'd be covered if I was off-base on your mood and you ended up accusing me of stalking."

"Aw, Jacob, I'm sorry too. For everything. You've been through an awful lot and it stinks." She dropped onto Al's back alongside Jacob and extended her hand. "You make a good partner, Jacob Brown."

The young man laughed as he held Al's head down to the pavement with his left hand and shook with his right. "So do you, Elise Jenkins. So do you."

TWENTY-SIX

8:55 a.m.
Monday, April 11

SHE FLIPPED ON the overhead light in the conference room, grateful to be back at work after a long and exhausting weekend. The stories she'd managed to file prior to the events of Friday morning made it into the Sunday paper. The ones she hadn't finished had been forced to wait.

Sam had stepped up to the plate in her absence, writing the news piece on the arrest of Al Nedley. And she'd been okay with that. The important thing was justice for Hannah, not the name on the byline that accompanied the breaking story.

But still, she'd be lying to herself if she didn't acknowledge the desire she had to finish Hannah Daltry's story. To expand the teacher's words to include an ending that resonated as loudly as the beginning.

"Well look who's here. Little Miss Kung Fu."

Without looking up, Elise set her notepad and pen on the table and sat down, her backpack purse gripped tightly in her lap. "Dare I ask?"

Dean took off in a run to the other side of the table, jumping the last few feet and landing with one arm extended outward, the other bent upward at the elbow. "Hiiiii-yaaa!"

She laughed. "What are you doing?"

He set his camera bag on the table and went back to a series of bizarre and dramatic arm motions. "I'm practicing up."

"For what? Stealing snacks from gorillas?"

"Nope." He clenched his jaw and threw out a leg to his side. "Just getting my war tactics down in case I stumble on a killer while eating scrambled eggs one morning."

Her head dropped into her palm, followed by a groan from somewhere deep inside her chest. "I didn't use Kung Fu. I just took a running jump and landed on an old guy's back. *That's it. Really.*"

The photographer stopped his uncoordinated motions, spun his chair around backwards, then straddled it so he was facing the table. "Does Mitchy know you do this kind of stuff? Or is that a topic better left behind closed doors."

She threw her pen at him and made a face.

"Elise…it's good to see you back. How are you feeling?"

Straightening in her chair, Elise looked up at her boss and smiled. "Thanks, Sam. I'm feeling great. Your story on the arrest was incredible—thanks for taking that for me."

"My pleasure. Once a journalist, always a journalist.

And there's no denying the adrenaline-surge that kicks in with a story like that. The funny thing is, if Nedley had just left Hannah alone, it's very likely he'd have been safe from his original crime thanks to exceeding the statute of limitations by thirty years. But now he's in for the rest of his life if he doesn't get executed first."

Elise flipped open her notepad and extracted a folded piece of paper she'd printed from her home computer over the weekend. "Actually, he can be tried with *both* crimes. If he'd stayed here in New Jersey after the robbery and not gotten caught, he'd have been free after five years. But, since he fled to Wyoming until six months ago, the statute of limitations was tolled. That means the five year clock started when he moved back." She wedged the printout between Sam's thumb and the top of his binder. "Pretty wild, huh?"

The editor scanned the highlighted paragraphs then handed the page back to her, pride etched in his face for his youngest reporter. "Nice work, Elise, very nice."

"Thanks, boss."

Sam grinned. "You know what was interesting? Everyone Nedley knew here was shocked he could do something so evil, so conniving. Madelyn being the angriest of them all."

Madelyn.

She'd almost forgotten all about her. "Is she okay?" Elise asked. "I think she kind of had a crush on him to be honest."

Sam nodded. "She'll be just fine. She's already

planning on writing a tell-all." He set his binder down with one hand, a large white paper bag with the other. "Hung—"

Tom bounded into the room, his yellow legal pad tucked under his arm. "Sorry I'm late. No hot water at my place this morning." He patted Elise's shoulder as he passed her chair. "You okay, sweetie?"

"She's fine," Dean answered with appropriate karate motions and sound effects before pointing at Sam. "What were you saying?"

"I was wondering if anyone was hung—"

"What's with all the cars in the parking lot?" Karen stood in the doorway, her face scrunched tightly. "Did we hire a second and third shift or what?"

"*People!* Our leader is trying to say something," Dean hissed through clenched teeth. "Let the man finish his sentence."

"*Is anyone hungry?*" Sam, Elise, Tom and Karen said in unison.

"That's better." Dean closed his eyes and reached his hands—palms upward—toward Sam and his bag. "Lay it on me, man."

Sam opened the bag and pulled out four large chocolate chip cookies from Ocean Point Bakery on Second Street. Elise sat up, raised a finger to her lips, opened her purse, and pulled out the Chips Ahoy! snack bag from last week.

Tom snorted.

Sam nodded the sports writer off and took the mini

bite-sized cookie from Elise. "Keep 'em closed there, big guy." He set a bakery cookie in front of himself and passed the other three on to Elise, Tom, and Karen. The miniature cookie was placed in Dean's hand. "Okay. There you go. Enjoy, everyone."

Dean opened his eyes and looked at the tiny why-bother cookie and made a face. "Is this it?"

"I propose a toast," Karen said suddenly. She raised her full-sized cookie into the air, prompting Elise, Sam, and Tom to do the same. Dean's mouth twisted as he looked down at his cookie forlornly and the society reporter continued. "To Elise's hard work and some much needed *mundane and boring* stories."

"Here, here," echoed Tom and Sam.

"Thanks, Karen." Elise pulled her cookie inward and winked at Dean as she slowly nibbled off a chocolate chip. "Mmmm, Sam, these are awesome. There's almost enough here for three meals."

Dean threw a karate chop in her direction then tossed the tiny cookie into his mouth, swallowing it whole. "Let's get this show on the road, shall we? I've got a desk to pillage."

"Okay, kids, Dean is right," Sam said, shivering from the top of his head down to his waist. "God, I didn't just say that, did I? Anyway, what's going on with Sierra McDermott?"

Elise stuffed the rest of the cookie bag into her purse and reached for her pen. "The community college is not pressing charges. They're thrilled that Hannah Daltry's murder has been solved so quickly, allowing them to move onto damage control that much faster."

"So nothing happens to her?" Tom asked, the shock evident in his hushed voice.

"I wouldn't say she's free and clear. She's got a serious image to live down now and she's offered to man the computer lab on the weekends for the next six months. Normally a paid position, the college will bring her on purely as a volunteer."

"And that's *punishment*?"

Elise turned to face the sports writer. "When it takes away her dream job at the bridal shop…yeah, it's punishment."

Tom shrugged, his expression still one of being unconvinced.

"The pressure that young lady is putting on herself is stronger than anything that anyone else can do, trust me," Sam interjected. "I talked to Jacob on Friday afternoon. He's standing by her."

"You saw Jacob again?" Elise asked her boss.

"Yes. He came by here looking for you."

"Me?"

Sam nodded. "Yup. He wanted to check on you. Make sure you were okay."

Swallowing over the lump that appeared in her throat at Sam's words, she simply nodded in response.

"That kid's going to be okay. He said he's been talking to Father Leahy and that writing his essay helped get some of his feelings out in the open." Sam pointed at an empty chair beside Dean. "In fact, he'll be occupying that chair on Monday mornings in about eight weeks."

She blinked against the sudden stinging in her eyes. God, she loved Sam…

"Why's that?" Dean asked.

"I offered him a summer internship with us. And he took it."

"You okay with that, Elise?" Tom asked suddenly.

Elise looked from Sam, to Tom, and back again, her voice shaky as it emerged from her lips. "I couldn't be any more okay with it. I think it's great."

She grinned in response to Sam's wink. Things were falling into place nicely. Except for one thing.

Narrowing her eyes, she glanced across the table at the photographer as he practiced martial arts moves with his fingers. "I got a strange call from my cousin, R.J. yesterday. Said he heard I've been stingy with the Nabisco products at work. Any idea where he'd get something like that?

Dean shrugged, his face reddening.

"What's the deal with you emailing all my friends and relatives?" Elise asked.

Dean pulled backward in his chair and motioned at his chest with shock and hurt. "Did *I* do that?"

She rolled her eyes. "Yes…"

"Go ask Debbie."

"What?" She stared at him as he opened his mouth and began digging trapped cookie crumbs from his molars.

He looked around the table slowly. "I think all that

Kung Fu on Friday damaged her hearing. I *said*…Go. Ask. Debbie."

Unsure of what to make of his odder-than-normal behavior, Elise looked to Sam for help.

Sam simply nodded and jerked his head toward the door.

"Oooo-kay." Pushing back her chair, Elise stood and walked out into the hallway that led to the receptionist's desk. As she got closer to her final destination, a menagerie of voices peppered the air. Loud voices, quiet voices, and everything in between.

She rounded the final corner between the conference room and the reception area and came to an abrupt halt. The subjects of the assorted photographs that dotted her apartment were standing around Debbie's desk, smiling at her.

Uncle Ken and Sophie.

Aunt Betty.

Jonathan.

Her cousin, R.J.

And Mitch.

A squeal escaped her mouth, causing a round of laughter from everyone as outstretched arms moved in her direction all at the same time. "Oh my gosh, what are you *doing here*?"

Six index fingers pointed behind her and she spun around, her gaze falling on a sheepish photographer with long, stringy blond hair and a Blue Oyster Cult concert t-shirt.

"Dean? You did this?"

"Yes, missy, I did. And that was *before* I knew you could beat the crap out of me if you wanted to."

Elise looked from Dean, to her loved ones, and back again, unsure of what to say.

"I've been working on this since the day you got back from Mackinac."

"What *is* this?" she finally asked.

"An engagement party!" everyone yelled together.

"Here? Now?"

"No, silly," Dean said, waving his hand in the air in dismissal of her ludicrous words. "That's tonight. At St. T's. But with everything you just went through, I figured you could handle seeing everyone *now*."

"But how? I just gave you the email addresses last week…"

"I'd waited too long to get back to everyone with hotel numbers and transportation options from the airport, so I decided to try that damn email you're always blabbering about."

"So the computer wasn't for," she felt her face grow warm, "viewing, um, weird sites."

Dean leaned against the wall and crossed his ankles. "Puh-lease. I like my women real."

"What women?" Mitch quipped.

Dean ignored him. "The postcards I mailed were just an extra touch I threw in to whet their appetite for the trip."

The lump from earlier appeared once again, only this

time it wasn't because of Sam. She held up her finger and disappeared down the hallway, returning seconds later with the cookie bag from her purse. "Here."

Grinning, he grabbed the blue bag from her hand and poured the contents into his mouth.

AS SHE LOOKED AROUND the room at her loved ones, Elise Jenkins knew—beyond a shadow of a doubt—that she was the luckiest woman in the world. Not only was she surrounded by the people she loved most, but they'd all come together to celebrate a promise she was about to make to the man of her dreams.

Her eyes instantly sought out Mitch as he stood in a corner talking to her uncle and Jonathan. There was something so strong, yet gentle…protective, yet loving about him as he looked up, mid-conversation, and smiled at her from across the room.

The butterfly brigade that lived in her stomach took flight as he excused himself from the group and headed in her direction.

It was still hard to believe that they'd be husband and wife in just a little over six months. On one hand it felt as if they'd just met—her heart rate still accelerating every time she saw him. On the other hand, it felt as if they'd known each other their entire lives.

And that's the way it was supposed to be.

She buried herself in his arms, reveling in the feel of his lips against her skin.

"Having fun?" he asked.

"Absolutely." Keeping one arm around him, she reached around his body to the blue folder she'd set beside her purse on the coat table. "I have something for you."

"Oh, yeah? What's that?" He popped his head up for a moment, then returned to kissing her forehead with gentle lips.

"My writing assignment…"

The kissing stopped and he stepped back, a grin spreading across his face like wild fire. "The one about me?"

She nodded. "Within the first few sentences, I knew it didn't fit the assignment we were given…but I kept on writing it anyway. Because it was what I wanted to say…what was—and is—in my heart."

"Do I get to read it now?" he asked as he reached for the folder.

"No. I want to read it to you."

Reaching for his left hand, she held the paper with her right. She didn't really need to read the printed words. They were forever embedded in her heart. But she read them anyway, her eyes meeting his from time to time as that infamous lump returned to her throat for the third time that day.

"What do you want to be when you grow up?"

It was a question I answered many times throughout my childhood regardless of who was asking. But unlike my peers, my answer never changed.

I wanted to be a writer.

I wanted to create worlds. I wanted to create

characters. I wanted to make people happy. Give them an escape.

But then I met you.

And suddenly my lifelong answer was different.

She paused, peered up at Mitch through tear-dappled eyelashes.

"What do you want to be when you grow up?" he asked, his voice huskier than normal.

"I want to be your wife. I want to create a world with *you.*"